£6.99

C000130856

Making Friends with the Crocodile

Mick Canning

Copyright © 2016 Mick Canning
All rights reserved.
Cover design and artwork by the author.
www.mickcanning.co

ISBN 9781729197226

DEDICATION

This book is dedicated to all of those numberless women, the victims of violence at the hands of men.

There is an Indian proverb that says: 'If you live by the banks of the river, you should make friends with the crocodile.'

ONE

What has caused me to be suddenly thinking about death?

It is quiet outside, and I am just beginning to drift off to sleep. Maajid is already snoring beside me. I don't recall anything unusual happening today, and I came to bed about a quarter of an hour ago feeling perfectly happy, or at least as happy as I usually am. I cannot imagine what could have brought up the thought of death in my mind, but now I am wide awake again as I wonder where it came from.

My home is in Nandiwar, a small village in Bihar, in northern India, similar to countless other villages nearby. I heard on the radio, maybe three or four weeks ago, that there are ten lakh villages in India! Just try to imagine that, if you can; ten lakh! A million! How can our country be large enough for a million villages to fit inside it? And then there are all of the towns and the cities to fit in, too. Patna is the city nearest to us. I have been there two or three times, and each time I felt lost and confused amongst all of the noise and the traffic and the masses of people there. When we had to cross over the main road, I was terrified that I was going to get knocked down. It seemed as though the traffic would never stop, even when the traffic lights had turned to red. And when they did change, and we walked quickly across the road in front of the cars and the lorries and the motorbikes, they seemed to me like a pack of savage animals that were growling and waiting for an opportunity to hurl themselves upon us and to tear us into pieces.

Maajid laughed at my fears, and called me a little country girl, but I saw that he also looked at everything with big, nervous eyes, and when we crossed the roads he ran across every bit as quickly as I did. I did not like it at all, and I could not wait to get back home to my village again. When I was a child, I thought that India was so large that there must be one lakh people living there. It seems that I did not know very much when I was a child.

My thoughts are drifting.

Occasionally, I wonder how old I am. My parents told me my age when I was a child, and I accepted that as naturally as I accepted everything else that they told me. There would be presents on my birthday; not big presents, naturally, for we were not well off and I wasn't a son, but presents nonetheless, and congratulations on reaching the age of seven or nine or eleven or whatever it might be. And then, when I had thought that I was thirteen, they told me that I was fifteen and so I was married to Maajid, bringing about a painful end to my innocence. That would make me thirty-nine or forty now, I forget which. Or maybe it is possible that I really am only thirty-seven or thirty-eight.

Once the sun is down, we eat. Tonight it is a scrawny chicken that Naira bought from the market. Oh Naira! I scold. Who has sold you that? Look at it! There is no meat on that! How are we all to eat that? *It was all there was*, she says sulkily, lowering her eyes. All there was? I am furious with her. I sent you out early. Where did you go? *I went to the market, of course.* She is surly, that one. She must have gone across the village to see her parents and sat drinking chai with them all morning instead of filling her basket at the market. Well, she will have the sinewy parts of the bird for her supper, and go to bed hungry tonight. Perhaps, then, she will carry out her duties with more care tomorrow.

In the event, of course, nobody goes to bed hungry. As well as the wretched chicken, there is rice and vegetables and bread. Sometimes I am tired, but Maajid will just say it doesn't matter. You only need lie there. I sometimes wish that he would be quieter, that he might not want others to overhear, but maybe he doesn't mind that because it he thinks that it shows them that I am his to do with as he will.

I suppose that all men are like that. My son must be like that with his wife. I picture Naira lying there and pouting while Tariq does his stuff with her. Not so loud she would mutter. Do you want your parents to hear you? *Let them* he would say, just the same as his father does. *I will do with you as I please.*

I am awoken most nights by a fox that comes past the house. I think that it is attracted by the cages of chickens in several of the lock-up stalls along the street. Its short, sharp barking reminds me of the trucks with huge loudspeakers that come around at electioneering time; Vote for me! It must be the tone, the timbre of the voice. Bark, bark, bark. Vote for me!

3

It is peremptory, an order. Vote for me. They are all foxes, those ones; so cunning. None of them are to be trusted. Vote for me and I won't eat you up. But they will, or they would do, if they could be bothered to take any interest in us after the election. But after they have been elected, they don't need us anymore. Not for another five years, anyway. And by then, with luck, they will have made enough from their contacts and contracts to retire somewhere on the proceeds.

Bark, bark, bark, and that sets off all of the other dogs in the village. No, vote for me, instead. What can they promise us if we do?

Even we women are allowed to vote; at least, to vote the way that we are told to vote. Maajid points out the symbols to me. There, the one with the ladder; that is the symbol of the Indian Union Muslim League. I am told that is because it is to help us Moslems to climb up and to get higher. Well, don't vote for them, because they'll never get in. There aren't enough of us. Do you understand? I nod. And this one – he jabs dismissively with his thumb – a lotus, supposedly. More like an umbrella on fire, if you ask me, well, that's the BJP. I nod again. He doesn't need to tell me who they are. But this one is the Congress Party; the hand in front of an Indian flag. Vote for them – they're the best of a bad bunch, as far as we are concerned.

I wonder idly whether he has been bribed. All of the parties do it, of course. A bottle of hooch here, a few rupees there. Naturally, though, I nod. I will do as I am told. But, once I am inside the ballot booth, who can say who I will vote for? And who will know?

A vehicle pulls up outside the house – something big. The engine is still running; a low, threatening growl, like a noise made by a large and dangerous animal.

Maajid stirs uneasily beside me, and I hear low voices now from the next room. After a few moments, though, there is a muttered goodbye and then a door slams heavily, metallically, and the engine roars again and the vehicle crunches its way along the road and then all that is left in the silence of the night are the slapping and shuffling sounds of feet fading away down the alleyway beside the house, which breathes and relaxes again.

An owl calls in the distance, and I cannot get back to sleep.

Long minutes pass; minutes that are drawn out into hours.

Outside, something goes clink. It sounds like a stone that has been disturbed by a foot, although I hear no footsteps. Perhaps the walker is barefooted. Maybe it is a housebreaker, creeping around in the darkness on the lookout for an un-shuttered window, or an opened doorway. I strain my ears to listen, but I can hear no further sounds. I am worried that if a housebreaker were to attempt to break in, then we would not know. There was a dog that lived in our yard until just four days ago, when it suddenly died. I went out in the early morning to find it lying in the dust, stiff and cold and twisted. Its back was arched and bent and I was sad, for it looked as though it had died in pain, and we had not known anything about it. But, I don't suppose that we would have been able to help the poor creature even if we had.

There was just that solitary clink, and now it is silent again outside. Who could possibly believe that there are so many millions of people out there?

And there it is again; this thought of death is worrying me. Maybe that is why I cannot get to sleep.

A little later, there is a low, steady, droning, and a motorbike passes beneath the window. It sounds like a fat, lazy fly going past aimlessly. But the rider must be going somewhere. I reach out and click the light on the top of my clock to see that it reads '11.47' and begin to wonder who it might be, who is up so late; who is going home so late. The shopkeepers around here will have locked and shuttered their stalls and gone home, if they lived elsewhere, hours ago. I think that perhaps it is a young man, who has been playing cards with his friends and, perhaps, drinking as well. I picture a group of them – four or five, maybe, sat beneath a tree in a yard and passing around a bottle from which they all take occasional but regular mouthfuls, shuddering slightly as they swallow the neat liquor that they are not really used to drinking yet, although each is trying hard not to let the others see that. They will be smoking as well, of course. Tariq is the only one in this house who smokes. He learned it from his friends. And these young men will be playing cards. What is it that they will be playing? I do not know the names of any card games, since they have always been forbidden to us. To women, I mean. Naturally, the men are not supposed to play, either, but they all do.

They will be playing cards, then. They will be playing for money, of course, for that is the reason that men play cards. They will be playing until the light fades too much for them to make out the shapes and numbers on the cards. And then, to avoid having too many arguments and, perhaps, coming to blows over these cards, they go indoors and arrange themselves on the floor in full view of the parents of the house, who are weak and indulgent and allow their son and his friends to take these liberties. There they sit and play until, perhaps, this young man on the motorbike has lost all of his money and so he gets up and takes his leave of his friends, who hardly notice his going, so wrapped up are they in their game, and he rides slowly and carefully across the village towards his home. Perhaps he is fearful of the reception that he will get from his father when he arrives home. *Where have you been? Do you know what the hour is?* Maybe he slinks off to his bed with muttered apologies, unable to meet his father's eye, but perhaps he is rude and insolent, like so many of the young men seem to be today. Perhaps he tells his father that it is none of his business, and that he will do what he chooses to do, and bad words are said, and his father threatens to throw him out of the house.

He goes past slowly, since the road is littered with rocks and pitted with holes. I wonder that he can see anything, but he must have a headlamp. As he neared the house I made out the faintest glow around the edge of the window, like the approaching dawn finding its way around the shutters, but the light was shaking and soon gone. Instead of silently and gradually seeping in, the way that the dawn light does, the juddering, jumping light seemed to be trying to force its way in, looking for weak spots. I am glad, for his sake, that he has a working headlamp on his bike. Often, I see drivers in the darkness whose lights do not seem to work and I am terrified for them that they will crash and perhaps kill themselves or some other person.

I picture the dust kicked up, choking and dense; the light from the headlamp lost in the choking clouds, but, of course, it would not be like that. The dust would be left behind, even while travelling slowly, not in front of the rider, hanging unseen and invisible in the still night air.

Maajid has a motorbike. At times, if he is in a good mood, he will take me into Kannapur, which is the name of our nearest town, to go to the shops there. Then he will go off to meet friends while I buy what I need to buy, and then I will go to find him where he is drinking chai and eating samosas and talking and laughing. I will have to plead with him to take me back and he will say *you go back, woman. It is only a couple of miles and I will pass you eventually and then I will give you a lift*, and he will wink at his friends and add *perhaps, if you have been good* and they will laugh, and I will go off feeling angry. Soon enough, though, I will hear the sound of the motor behind me and turn round, and then he will stop beside me and I will say *oh, so you have decided to come home, then* and he will smile, but say nothing except maybe *come on, then, if you want a lift* and we will drive back amicably enough.

I turn over, restlessly. Tonight seems to be an exceptionally long night, and something is worrying me, something more than just the thought of death, perhaps.

As we live hundreds of miles from the coast, I have never seen the sea, at least not in real life. I have seen it on the TV, naturally, usually in the background while a group of choreographed girls dance and sing a popular song, or a rugged hero – who is always so white, why is everyone on the TV so white? Are we Indians supposed to be ashamed of our colour? – a rugged hero defeats a group of armed thugs (and they will be of a darker colour, for some reason). Every shout and blow and scream will be especially loud, and filmed in close up and slow motion, or even if the camera is simply focused on a couple of people who are talking, then their every utterance will require dramatic bursts of music and exaggerated expressions, so it is a wonder that anyone notices the backdrop scenery at all.

But I love the sea. I would love to go to the coast one day. I did see the River Ganges, one time that we visited Patna, and the river is so wide there that I thought we must have somehow reached the coast. Standing there and looking across to the other side, I felt that I was staring over to another country; another country that was also somehow still India. And it is so wide that I am told that there is a bridge near there that crosses the river and that it is the longest bridge in the world, and I can well believe it. I have never seen it, though.

Maajid lies beside me, and I think that his snoring must be like the sea – the sea that I have not yet seen, and probably never will. He breathes in, and the sound reminds me of the waves running out over the shingle while when he then breathes out again, it is the gentle breaking of a wave coming in. But then he catches his breath; there is a low rumble somewhere in his throat, he smacks his lips and mutters something that I cannot hear, and then turns over and lies soundlessly for a few minutes until he has settled, and then the snoring begins again. It seems to be a long, long time after this that I finally manage to fall asleep.

As soon as there is the faintest light, it is no longer night time, and so it is time for me to get up. But this morning I am tired. I have not slept well. I lie still and look around the room, and now I can make out shapes that are patches of a deeper blackness in the heavy gloom. There is a large metal trunk beneath the window, where

I keep my clothes and a few of my other possessions. It is most important to me, this trunk, as it was all that I brought with me when I married Maajid. When Maajid married me, I should say. Women do not marry men, men marry women. My parents gave me this trunk to keep my clothes in and it is a reminder of them to me, every time that I look at it. I do not have any photographs of them, for my father would not allow any to be taken. For that reason, too, there are no photographs of me taken before I was married.

Quietly, I rise from the bed, throw a shawl around my shoulders, and go across to the doorway. I push aside the curtain that covers it, slip my sandals on, and step out into the courtyard. Outside, everything is cold and grey. I can make out few colours other than those of the four bright plastic chairs that stand about randomly on the beaten earth. All the other colours are pale and drab next to their shining, gaudy red. As I walk past one of them, I idly run my finger along the hard, smooth surface, smearing the damp dust that has settled there. The morning fog hangs low over the houses, muffling all of the sounds that I would otherwise hear at this time of the day. All that I hear is the slap of my sandals on the ground.

We have a latrine in the yard. I use that, and then I take my toothbrush which sits with the others in an old cup on a shelf outside the kitchen, I unbolt the courtyard gate, and walk outside. A few yards along the street there stands a water pump. It is a large, brown, metal pump with a long, slightly curved arm that takes quite a lot of strength to use. Once, there was a low wall of mud bricks that surrounded it, so that the water that was not caught in pots or pans would collect in a small lake that small children could play in, or cows and goats would come to drink from, unless it was filled with clothes that were being washed. But the bricks are now broken and gone, so that when the pump is used the water flows this way and that in tiny streams and collects in small puddles that are of no use to anyone except for the thirsty animals, and then it gets trampled into mud and spread along the street by feet and bicycles and wagon wheels, since no one seems to be interested in replacing the bricks.

Along the street a dog barks. Nearby, a neighbour is already sweeping the dust and leaves from outside her doorway, while her neighbour lights the fire that she will use to boil water on, right at the edge of the street. Her husband sits in the doorway; a blanket wrapped tightly around his shoulders, puffing furiously on a beedi, the poor cheap cigarettes that many of the men in the village smoke. Here and there, already several small fires are smoking at the roadside, as householders burn the dried leaves and scraps of rubbish that they have swept up. Nobody speaks. I finish brushing my teeth and rinse out my mouth, at the same time as the smoker nearby clears his throat and spits. His neighbour's brush still rasps harshly on the ground, raising small clouds of dust despite the dampness. There is the urgent sound of a horn in the distance, and finally voices from the house behind where I am standing. Wiping my face with the edge of my shawl, I walk across the street and back into the yard.

Unusually, this morning, I am not the first to rise. When I return from the pump I attempt to light the fire. Naira has already tried, but has been unable to get the damp twigs to catch. Later, I will go to Maajid and I will complain; I will say where did you find this fine lady, this princess, for our son? She does nothing except eat our food, which I have to cook anyway, for every time that I trust her to cook it, then it is burned because she is gossiping with her friends at the gate or painting her nails and she does not have any idea what to look for when I send her to buy food, and the storekeepers send her away with the scrawniest chicken or with vegetables that are rotten and they overcharge her at the same time and she has *still* not produced for us a grandson...And he will tell me so train her, then. The kitchen is your domain, woman. Do not bring your petty squabbles to me. And as for the grandson, then we must pray to Allah.

We have said all this many times before.

This morning there are eggs. I shall fry a couple for Maajid, for he loves them that way; soft and greasy. But first, Naira must fetch water so that we can make the chai. Already, the fog has lifted and almost disappeared, and her plump shadow moves before her as she goes out of the gate and across the street towards the pump. Her footsteps stop, and now I hear the sounds, half creaking and half squeaking, and the whoosh of water in the pot, as she works the handle of the pump. When she returns, the pot is balanced on her head, although she needs to use both hands to keep it steady, and I can see that she is fearful of dropping it.

When first she came to live in our house - the very first morning that she was here - I sent her out for water and when she returned with it, she was lifting it off of her head at the same time that she was walking in through the doorway of the kitchen, and carelessly she let the pot slip through her hands. When it hit the ground, the contents shot across the kitchen in a jet of water that both doused the fire and also soaked me to the skin. I remember being shocked, and the look of shock also on Naira's face, and then my fury and my shouting – I don't remember what I said – and then Tariq and Maajid were at the doorway and looking at me, and they were laughing. I looked at them for a moment, and then I slapped Naira very deliberately, and pushed past the men and went to change. When I came back to the kitchen the men had gone and there was another pot of water sitting on the floor, and Naira was squatting in front of it, her eyes lowered, but the fire had not been re-lit, which only made me angry again, but this time I was mindful of the proverb that says that anger is a stone cast into a wasps' nest, and so I merely said 'Light the fire again and we will make the chai.'

I have lit the fire. At least Naira had put aside the ashes for cleaning the plates and the pots before she attempted to light it earlier. It took me a while, for the few twigs that she used that had been sitting against the wall in the kitchen were damp, and the fire would not take hold. I had wasted several matches before the flames suddenly crackled and leapt upwards and began to creep along the twigs. Once I am happy that it has taken, I break a dung cake in half and put it on the fire. When this has taken, I carefully place another couple on top and then sit back on my haunches. 'Where is the water?' I ask. 'Here,' she says, and hands me the pan. I put it over the flames and tell Naira to get the tea and the tin of masala that we keep just for making chai, and to add them to the water.

Once the tea is boiling, she opens a tin of milk and pours in the contents, and finally breaks off a lump of sugar from the block that is kept in a tin on the top shelf, and stirs it all into the chai. She looks up then, and sees me standing by the doorway watching her. Her eyes meet mine, and now she looks at me resentfully. 'You can start making the chapattis now,' I say.

For a moment she does not move, and I think that she is about to speak, but then she turns and crosses the kitchen to reach up to the top shelf where the tub of ghee lives. I watch her taking it down, waiting to see whether she dares to answer me back, and I catch myself thinking that at least it is fortunate that she is tall. And then I am thinking that as well as being tall, her hands are noticeably larger than mine and then her hips, too, will be good for childbearing, but then I start to feel angry that she has not yet done so, and so I turn my back on her again.

Maajid sits there, blinking into the morning sun, saying nothing, sipping his chai. The radio is on, but too low for me to make out more than a low buzz of voices. The little metal and plastic box stands on the ground close beside one leg of his chair, bringing him news of places that he has never been to and can hardly imagine. He listens intently, and frowns occasionally, or nods every now and again when he hears news about a person or a place that he has heard of before. His concentration is interrupted briefly as I drop a metal plate, just outside the kitchen.

'Quiet, woman,' he says, but softly, without rancour. He does not even bother to glance in my direction. It is the voice of authority. He knows, and I understand, that he need not raise his voice to me, for I shall obey him. I think it more demeaning than if he did so. It means that he knows that it is certain that I will obey him. And so, I obey. In a society where it is dangerous to think too much, you learn to guard your tongue.

'Did you hear that, they shot those villagers? Animals!' But there is no heat in his voice, and it is unclear whether it is the villagers or the soldiers that he refers to as animals. And I do not really know what he thinks, even after all of these years. Sometimes he will say one thing, and at another time he may say some other thing, seemingly the opposite of some view that he has already expressed.

And he expects no answer, for he is not telling it to me, but to himself. Did you hear that, Maajid? Did you hear what they did to those villagers? And why did they shoot them, anyway? What had they done? Were they rebels? And does it matter to me? Most importantly, does it matter to me?

Already, the pattern of the day has been established.

TWO

'Mother! I do not have a clean shirt!'

'And why are you telling that to me? Go to your wife and tell her that your shirts are not clean.'

'I do not understand why we cannot send our clothes to the Dhobi. We should then have them clean when we wanted them.'

'So who is going to pay the Dhobi Wallah? Can you afford it? Will you pay for them out of your wages?'

'Mama!'

'Not now, Leila!'

Leila is my youngest daughter.

'I would if I could afford to, but I would rather that the women of this house took just a little more care in their duties!'

'Siddiqa!'

And I am Siddiqa. I know that I have not introduced myself properly, yet, and I apologize for that, but you can see that there is no time at the moment. You will get to know me in the same way as you will come to know the others in my family; by watching them and listening to them. I have already told you quite a lot...

'Siddiqa! Bring me more bread!'

'So what am I to wear today?'

'Mama!'

'Leila, be *quiet!* Go and ask Naira what you will wear, Tariq.'

'Am I to wait forever for bread?'

'Naira! *Naira!* Where are you? Take your father in law some more bread! Now, what do you want, Leila?'

I cannot find my sandals, Mama. I will be late for school.'

'Oh, Leila! Surely you must know what you have done with your shoes?'

'No, Mama, I'm sorry, Mama, Have you seen them?'

'Why would I have seen them? Are they not beside your doorway? Go and look again.'

'Yes, Mama.'

'And Leila...*Leila!* Where are your books?'

'Here, Mama, in my room, with my satchel and...oh, my sandals!'

Tariq has his clean shirt – I have no idea where he found it, presumably Naira found it for him – and he has his briefcase, and even though he is a married man, I still find it hard not to smile with motherly pride as I see him standing there.

Today, Tariq will have a lift from Maajid, who is off to Kannapur on the motorbike, to work for the day in the shop of his brother, Shamil, who is a carpenter. It is not every day that he has work, and so he is in a good mood. Shamil mainly makes furniture, but will turn his hand to most things. When he is busy, he will frequently ask Maajid to help him out. Maajid tells me that he will mostly be asked to plane and sand the wood, or to roughly cut the planks and logs into shape for Shamil to work. Occasionally he will need to polish one of the finished pieces. For this Shamil will pay him a good wage, as well as paying for his lunch, and I wish that Shamil could give him work every day, for families should look after their own. As they go, I hear an auto pull up outside the gate, and then a most distinctive horn sounds. To me, it sounds like a hoarse squeak, but Maajid says that it sounds like a wet fart.

'Leila, he is here! Where is your sister? Hana! Daanish is here now!'

There are already four little girls crammed into the auto by the time that it reaches our gate, and now they all have to squeeze up further so that Leila and Hana may fit in beside them. Each gives the driver a one rupee coin, which he tucks into his pocket without any acknowledgement, and they set off slowly, also for Kannapur.

And now there are only Naira and myself left at the house. Although I can hear the noise and bustle from outside in the street, it seems relatively quiet and calm. There is still hot water in the pan on the cooker, and so I make chai for us and call Naira out from wherever she is skulking in the house, so that we can decide on what she needs to go out and buy for our supper tonight. We will have mutton, I decide, and I tell her again not to go to the stall run by old Manit, who claims that his meat is halal meat, although this is doubted by the majority of the women in the village.

'And then we must have a couple of cauliflowers, and some more rice. Oh, and some eggs and onions. You can carry all of those, can't you? It isn't too much.' But then I decide 'No, I have changed my mind. I will go and get those, while you clean the breakfast things. And when I come back we must do the washing.'

This does not please Naira, who no doubt had been looking forward to a walk across the village to visit her parents first, or at least to spending some time gossiping with her friends, but I take a basket and I go out of the gate, and leave her in the yard gathering together the dishes and the ash and preparing to go over to the pump. Just before I turn down the street, I call back to remind her to close the gate before she does that, and then I am walking in the morning sunshine and the cold of the night has gone and the birds are singing and I am smiling and saying good morning to everyone that I meet.

When I get back, I leave the basket in the kitchen for Naira to unpack, and go to sort out the clothes that need to be washed. I cross the yard and walk into our room and the first thing that I see is my trunk, my precious trunk, lying on its side across the bedroll with the lid open and bent at a strange angle with one hinge broken and the contents strewn out across the floor and over the bedroll and in little heaps here and there.

'Naira!' I scream, 'What has been going on in here?'

I am on my knees in an instant, picking up my undergarments and looking for my rings and bracelets as Naira arrives at the doorway. She draws her breath in sharply and loudly – too loudly, I think. It seems to be for my benefit. I notice this even as I am on my hands and knees looking for my jewellery. For the moment, she does not speak. I can feel myself on the very edge of crying, and that makes me feel angrier yet, and so I do not trust myself to speak.

After a moment I feel Naira at my side, and she, too, drops to her knees and then picks up a sari and begins to fold it. She finishes this and puts it down and then begins to fold another as I search the room for my jewellery. My jewellery! Where is my jewellery? There is none left in the trunk; I crawl into the corners of the room and feel inside cracks in the floor and feel under all the edges of the bedroll and amongst the boxes and bags on the floor and I look around wildly and I know that my eyes are wide open and scared. After a few minutes have gone by, there is a pile of neatly folded clothes on the bedroll and I am sitting back on my haunches looking at the single ring in my hand that is all that I have managed to find.

'They have gone! They have gone! They have been stolen!' I burst into tears.

'Amma,' says Naira softly, 'what are you missing?'

'My jewellery! All my jewellery is gone! Someone has got into the house while I was out! How did they get in? How could you not see them, Naira? How could you not see them?' There is no reply, and then;

'I am so sorry,' she whispers. 'I forgot to pull the gate across when I went to the pump.'

Naira's sudden contrition and honesty take me completely by surprise. I stop crying and stare at her, as now she lowers her head and begins to cry, too.

'I am so, so, sorry, Amma!' And then suddenly she is wringing her hands and wailing and rocking backwards and forwards on her knees. 'It is all my fault!' She raises her head now and looks into my face, and I see that her eyes are wild and haunted and I have never seen her like this before, and it scares me slightly. '*Everything* is my fault!'

'Stop it, Naira!' But she continues to wail and rock, although now she does not take her eyes from mine. Her lips are parted slightly, and I can just see the tips of her teeth.

'Naira!' The wailing becomes louder. 'That will do! Stop it now!' I half raise my hand as if to slap her, and as I do her eyes open unnaturally wide and she bares her teeth and, her eyes still locked on mine, sinks the nails of both hands into her face, slowly raking them down both cheeks and, horrified and fascinated and scared, I watch the blood trickling down her face and it seems to be trying to catch up with her fingers but by the time that it begins to drip from her face and onto her lap her hands are clenched in the air before her, and she is staring blankly into my face through me...past me...

And now she begins to retch, helplessly tipping forward onto her hands and knees. Her eyes are squeezed shut and her mouth gapes wide open and her tongue protrudes slightly and her whole body strains as each spasm of coughing produces nothing but noise and anguish and tears and when it subsides a little she manages to get to her feet and then she staggers unsteadily out of the doorway. As the curtain falls back behind her, I see drops of her blood on the floor and on the blanket where I am still kneeling, clutching my one remaining ring. I realize that I am shaking.

Seconds later, I hear her scream again. 'Amma! Amma! Come quickly!'

I find that I cannot move at first, but then I force myself to get to my feet and I go warily out into the yard.

Naira stands at the entrance to the latrine, blood dripping from both cheeks, but her eyes are bright with excitement.

'Look!' She points through the doorway and there, scattered across the floor of the latrine, are my rings and bracelets. Oh, this is a puzzle indeed! I stare through the doorway and then take one step forward, hesitate, glance at Naira to see that she, too, is still staring at the jewellery, and then I stride in, bend down and gather them up in my hands. When I stand, I am clutching them tightly to my chest as if afraid that even now, a robber might appear to take them from me.

I turn around to face Naira, and am relieved to see that her face no longer has that mad, staring intensity of a few moments before. She seems to sag slightly and then raises her hand to the side of her face and looks at the blood, puzzled.

'What happened? Did you do that to me?'

'No.' I look at her hands. 'Look at your fingernails, Naira.' Without moving her hand, she curls her fingers gently and studies her nails.

'I did it?' She is astonished. I nod. 'Why did I do that?'

'I do not know, Naira. You were...not yourself. It was as if a demon spoke through you, as though you were possessed.' We stand for what feels like a long time, looking at each other without speaking.

'Your jewellery?' I understand the cryptic question.

'Come and see.' She follows me into our room and I have the strangest feeling as she sets eyes on the scene there and draws her breath in sharply – I am afraid that everything is going to repeat itself, but she merely asks 'What happened?'

'This is what I found when I came home. But, leave it for now, Naira. Leave it. Let me bathe your face.' I put my jewellery down onto the bedroll, and then we go to the kitchen. I tell Naira to go and find some clean cloth while I put a pan of water back over the fire. I understand that the water needs to have boiled if I am to clean her wounds properly. When she returns with the cloth, which seems to take her a surprisingly long time, I see that she has been crying again so I do not say anything about it but take the cloth and tell her just sit down, over there, and I dip the edge of the cloth into the water and hold it for a moment or two so that it can cool down a little, and then I clean up her face. The blood has almost dried, so that at least it does not begin to bleed again when I do so, and it does not take long to wipe off the dried blood, and then I say 'There, it is done. Just be certain to keep your scarf around your face so that no one sees it.'

'Thank you,' she says quietly. 'We had better do the washing now.'

'You start,' I say. 'I have not finished in our room.' and I do not mention it again to her.

I go and pick up the trunk with the broken hinge, but at least the lid will sit on the top without sliding or tipping and so I can still use it. Perhaps the hinge can be mended another time. I put away my folded clothes and, after some hesitation, my jewellery, too, and gather together my other small possessions that had been scattered around the room, then close the lid. I then look at the window which has the shutters open but has bars across, and I think no one could have got in that way. It must have been through the gate in the yard, and so yes, it is certainly Naira's fault for not closing it behind her, but I am not going to mention it again, for she frightened me, that one, when she did that. I know that everybody is going to think that it was me that scratched her face, even if she tells them that it

23

was her, for why should she do such a thing? Indeed, why should she?

I gather together the clothes of mine and of Maajid that need to be washed and I go out to join Naira at the pump, making sure that I pull the gate across behind me. There is already a neighbour there with her own washing and she and Naira are chatting away as they work. She does seem to get on easily with all of the neighbours, I think. As I reach them Naira looks up and smiles, but then she continues with what she is doing and she continues chatting to her friend, so I squat down and help with the washing. As each garment is finished, I wring it out and when a few are done, I carry them back to the house. I go in through the gate, and then throw the clothes up on top of the roof of the veranda, and step up on a chair and reach up and pull them out this way and that so that they lie flat and can dry in the sun. By the time that the last one is done I can already see the first ones steaming, and then I go back out and get the next pile.

Later, in the afternoon, both of the girls have returned from school and are nagging at me to help them with their homework. I tell Naira to start grinding the spices for the supper this evening, and then go and sit with the girls on the edge of the veranda in the shade. Hana has mathematics and English, and we do the mathematics first, because I am quite good at arithmetic, and so it will not seem too strenuous. I sit with my back against one of the poles that supports the veranda roof, watching while Hana carefully writes out each sum and then works it out and writes in the answer and then says after each one: 'Is that right, Mama?' And I say 'Yes, that's good' or, occasionally,' I don't think so, perhaps you should work it out again' and she pouts indignantly but with a smile and gets out her rubber and rubs out the offending sum and tries again.

When she has finished, she shows me her English assignment and I look doubtfully at it and say 'Well, have a go at it, and I will have a look, but you know that I only have a few words of English and won't be able to help you much, so if you think it's wrong then you must wait until Tariq comes home. When he has had a rest you must ask him nicely, that's nicely, mind, and perhaps he will help.' and Hana says 'Alright, thank you, Mama.' Then Leila says 'My turn now! I also have mathematics, and I have geography. Shall we do the mathematics first?' 'Yes, we'll do that,' I say, and she lies down on the veranda with her exercise book open in front of her, waving her legs slowly in the air backwards and forwards, with her pencil in her hand and her tongue sticking out of the side of her mouth, which is what she always does when she is trying to concentrate. I say 'That does not help, you know,' and she says 'I don't do it deliberately, Mama', and closes her mouth, but a few moments later it is sticking out again, and I smile but say nothing.

When they have finished their homework, I send them into the kitchen to help Naira, because it is important that they know what to do in the kitchen. Maajid always says 'I don't know why we bother sending them to school, because they will only get married, and they will not need that learning then, will they? So what is the point of it all?' But he does take some interest in what they do, and he asks them 'What did you learn today?' and he listens to their answers and smiles and says 'You're my clever little girls!' and hugs them, and so I do not think that he really minds their going at all. And I think it is important that they learn things because I never really had the chance to, and maybe there will be more choice in their lives when they grow up than I have had, but I keep those thoughts to myself.

The sun is setting when Maajid and Tariq return from the town. I hear the sound of the motorbike before they reach the gateway, and I think it is strange that I know it is them, because there are many other people with motorbikes in the village, but I know that is ours. I suppose that it must be something to do with the sound that it makes, something that I recognize without knowing that I do, and I am right, it is them. Maajid parks the bike just outside the latrine, pushing down the stand with his foot and leaning it gently over, still holding the handlebars firmly until he is certain that the stand has taken the weight of the machine, and then he lets go. I know that he always does that; I know that he is fearful that it will fall over and damage the bike, and he will not be able to afford to have it repaired, but I do not let him know that I know that.

Tariq comes into the kitchen to greet Naira and me and when he has said hello he looks at Naira and says 'What is this? Show me your face.' And he pulls aside the scarf from around her face.

'It is nothing,' she says, and avoids looking at me.

''No, it is not nothing. How did you get these?' And Maajid has now also come into the kitchen and I see him out of the corner of my eye leaning against the doorway, but for the moment he says nothing. 'Are you going to tell me?' Tariq says to Naira, raising his voice.

She looks at him and says 'It was me, I did it. I'll tell you later. I need to attend to this food if you want to eat tonight.'

So Tariq looks across at me now and says 'Mother? What is this?'

'She is telling you the truth, Tariq. Let her finish what she is doing,' I say, but this doesn't please him, and he purses his lips and walks past me and Maajid out into the courtyard, and for a moment I wonder if I should follow him, but decide it is best if Naira speaks first, so that he does not think that I am hurrying to tell him my side of the story first.

'I have had a busy day and I do not need this,' says Maajid, 'but come with me and tell me what has been going on.' And we go out into the courtyard and then into our room and before Maajid can say anything I go over to my trunk and lift the broken lid.

'See this? I came home this morning to find my trunk knocked over and my jewellery gone.'

'You what?' Maajid says.

'Yes, Naira had left the gate open when she went to the pump,' I reply.

'And your jewellery has been taken?' he says.

'Yes, but the strangest thing is that we found it again, or Naira found it.'

'Naira found it?' Maajid looks as though he does not believe any of it but he looks again at the broken lid of the trunk and says 'Where did she find it?'

'In the latrine.'

'In the latrine? So you have your jewellery back.'

'Yes.'

'And Naira's face?'

'She did it herself,' I say, and attempt to describe those strange minutes to Maajid. He hears me out without interrupting, but I can tell that he does not believe it.

'And the jewellery was in the latrine?' he asks again.

'Yes.' I say. 'I know that is strange but that is where it was.'

'Why would it be in the latrine?'

'I do not know, but there it was.' He scratches his chin thoughtfully.

'Well if you say that is what happened, then it must have been so. You must make sure that Naira knows to close the gate every time. But I am worried if she did that to her face. Why would she do that?'

'She was very upset,' I say, but he snorts and waves a hand dismissively.

'Well I get upset sometimes, but I don't do that to my face.' I don't reply and for a moment we look at each other warily and then he says 'We had better go and eat.'

THREE

The moon is sinking, and its last rays provide me with only the faintest illumination as they sneak through the slats of the shutters. At any moment now, it will disappear behind the houses on the other side of the street and then the darkness in the room will be complete. I love the moonlight, though. I always think of it as a pure white light; the purest light, purer indeed than sunlight. Perhaps this was the light that God originally created; a perfect, colourless light, perpetually lovely but always cold as a counterpoint to the fierce, mad heat of the daytime. I know many people say that the light of the moon can cause madness, but just to see it relaxes me and gives me a feeling of calm. Gold causes madness in men, too, but the moon is the colour of silver. I think that it is the sun that causes madness.

It is an old moon, tonight, giving off very little light to aid any walker who might still be abroad at this time. In two nights it will have completely disappeared, and then it will be another couple of nights before we see the first thin crescent of the new moon, looking as though someone had opened a strange, curved door just a crack, just an inch or two, to let out the tiniest amount of light from inside the unknowable room beyond that door, but what a bright light it seems!

I have not often walked in the moonlight, but once I came back from the town at the dead of night and in the light of the full moon. Everywhere, there was silence. It was winter, as it is now, and away from the houses and the road, a very faint mist hung in the air just above the empty fields. It felt colder than usual, and I was walking quickly to try to keep warm. My eyes were on the road, because I was scared that there might be snakes waiting there, sleepy and dangerous. In the night time, and especially in the colder months, they love to lay on the paths and the roads at night, taking advantage of the heat from the day that remains there. Although the air feels chilly, if you can find it in you to pause in your walk and stoop down and feel the ground, then the earth and, especially, the stones feel warm to the touch even at that time of night.

But that night, there was a silver light painted over the roads and fields. It sparkled on the edges of palm leaves that were otherwise like black sword blades hanging like threats in the night over me. It had been soaked up by the mist and sprinkled into the dust on parked motorbikes and sleeping dogs. It glistened on a buffalo that watched me pass by and I felt, I knew not why, that I should raise my hands in the air and shout with joy. There were shadows; deep, long shadows like the sun would have cast, but in a cold, pale white and silver so that, for some reason, the contrast between light and dark was confused and uncertain. I felt that I was walking through a magical, sleeping land.

The moon has gone, and the darkness is now complete. I think of the motorcyclist of the previous night, and how he could find his way in the dark with the lamp on the front of his machine, and of how hard it is to walk in the pitch black. Now that the moon has set, I know that if I was attempting to make my way along the street outside, even though it is so familiar to me, I would be walking slowly and nervously as I tried to ensure that I did not trip over rocks or potholes. Sleepy now, I find myself walking along that very road and looking over my shoulder to make sure that I am not being followed. My mother walks beside me, which surprises me, but I know better than to say anything which will upset her and so I hold my tongue. But the car that I had been long dreading, without actually realizing it, suddenly roars out of the darkness behind us and I am terrified, both for myself and for my mother and, involuntarily, I scream, although I immediately bite my lip, but it is no good, she has heard me and it disturbs her and she begins to walk away from me just as I wake up.

Maajid stirs uncomfortably in his sleep, muttering quietly as if in response to my dream. Otherwise, it is still and silent. Even without the moon, I love the peace of the night. I have time to explore my thoughts and to build a completely different world to that which I inhabit during the day. There are no tasks to do or people to please or to offend. No one is demanding that I do this or that for them. Tonight I am thinking of my jewellery lying scattered across the latrine floor.

Maajid groans and rolls over and I turn my head towards him, although I cannot make out any shapes in the darkness. I remember now his greed at the evening meal tonight, and wonder whether he might be in pain.

His breathing seems a little more laboured than is usual; heaven knows, I listen to it every night, and I should be able to tell. Outside, a car drives past slowly. I vaguely hear the creak of its springs as it bounces over the uneven surface of the road, but I am only really listening to the sounds that Maajid is making. He is clearly uncomfortable, but at the moment he still seems to be asleep. What should I do? I wonder. Should I get up and boil some water? There will still be hot embers in the cooking fire that I can use.

I get up and feel my way to the doorway. Outside, there is just enough light from the stars for me to make my way across the courtyard without bumping into anything or tripping over. It is bitterly cold, and I can see my breath in the air in the faint starlight. Just before I reach the kitchen a dog nearby begins barking, no doubt at hearing the sounds of my hesitant footsteps, and this is soon taken up by several other dogs. On the floor inside the kitchen there sits a kerosene lamp and I reach for the matches from the shelf and strike one which flares so brightly that for a moment I am unable to see anything, but I hold the light away from me and after a moment I can see enough to be able to raise the glass of the lamp and light the wick.

There had been no glow from the ashes of the fire when I entered the kitchen, but now that I hold my hand over the top of them I can feel a heat rising and, with the lantern standing on the floor beside the cooker, I kneel and blow gently at the embers, which soon begin to glow bright orange. I pause, and a few flames flicker and take hold on the last, half burnt pieces of wood and dung. In the corner is some wood, and I build up the fire a little and wait for the fresh wood to catch. I need some water, but I am a little reluctant to unbolt the gate and go to the pump, so I look around the kitchen and am relieved to find a pot that is almost half full. More than enough for what I need.

While the water is heating up, I take the lantern and go back to see how Maajid is. I can hear him groaning even before I reach the doorway, and as I push the curtain aside he murmurs irritably 'Where have you been? I am in agony.' I hold the lamp up, and look down at him. He is lying on his back, with his knees bent up and his hands clasped across his stomach.

'Have you a stomach ache?' He looks at the light and now I see also that his forehead is gleaming with sweat.

'A dreadful one. That mutton must have been bad.'

'I don't think so. You seem to be the only one with the stomach ache. I have put some water on and I will make you a drink for the pain. It won't be very long.'

Back in the kitchen, I am looking through jars and tins, trying to find all of the ingredients that I want. We have most of them, although the mint has dried out and I think that it will not be as good as it would be if it was fresh, but it will have to do. Holding the lamp over the pot of water, I see that it is now beginning to boil and so I drop all of the ingredients into it.

I should really leave the drink to boil for longer, but I am becoming worried about Maajid and want to give it to him as soon as possible, and so after just a few minutes I tip some of the drink into a mug and carry it across the yard to our room.

'What is this?'

'Mint and cumin and ginger and a few other things. They are all good for your stomach. Drink it.' He sits with difficulty and I kneel behind him as he sips, supporting his shoulders. 'When you have drunk that I will get some more; the next one will be stronger.'

We remain like this until he has finished the mug, and then I take it from him and help him to lie back down again. When I return with the mug refilled, his groans have become louder and he is rolling around on the mat. As I pause in the doorway, Tariq appears at my shoulder.

'Naira woke me. What is happening?'

'Your father has a very bad stomach ache. Maajid, here is the drink. I will help you to sit up.' I give the lamp and the mug to Tariq to hold and kneel down beside my husband. But Maajid will not remain still for long enough for me to help him, and in the lamplight I see that his eyes are bulging like those of a frog.

'Oh...this pain...it is too bad!' he gasps.

'Do you need to go to the latrine?'

'Possibly...I don't know...'

'Come on, then. Tariq, help me. Take his other arm.' We help him to stand, and take his weight as we guide him out of the doorway into the yard. He seems to be unable to work out where he is going, and is struggling to stay on his feet, but eventually we get him to the latrine. Once he is inside, Tariq puts the lamp down on the floor beside him, and pulls the curtain across the doorway. I wait nervously just outside, while Tariq goes out to get some water from the pump. Almost immediately, Maajid calls out weakly;

'Help me, Siddiqa.' Quickly I pull aside the curtain.

'What is the matter?'

'I can't keep my balance.' He seems irritated by this, but I put my hands on his shoulders to steady him and he actually smiles slightly. 'What a thing to have to do.'

'It does not matter,' I reply quickly. 'Who else would do it for you?'

After a while he says simply 'Nothing's happening. Help me up.' But as soon as he has managed to get to his feet he lurches away from me and is violently sick. Then he straightens up and says weakly 'That feels better.'

'Perhaps the poison is gone, now. Come on, I'll get you back to bed. This night air is cold.'

But he no longer needs my assistance, and walks back on his own. Once he is in our room, I take the lantern again and go out to clean up. Tariq has already gone back to his room, and I am alone with my thoughts.

FOUR

This morning the sky is a pale, clear blue and there is a thin ice on the puddles around the pump across the street. Ice! The girls are excited and fascinated. Hana tells me that the temperature must be at exactly zero degrees, and then rushes out after Leila and joins her at the pump. At first, they are touching the ice gently and carefully, as if they are afraid it is like glass and will easily shatter, but soon they are trying to prise up pieces of it from out of the frozen ground. It is indeed very thin and it shatters easily, but finally they manage it and then they are licking pieces like ice lollies, and giggling until they start to shiver and rub their hands together. Then Leila comes running back to warm her hands at the cooking fire, but when I look out Hana has taken off her sandals and is standing in one of the icy puddles with her face screwed up and her head thrown back and her arms sticking out and her fingers spread wide. 'Come in you foolish girl!' I say, but she either doesn't hear me or she chooses to ignore me in the grip of this strange ecstasy.

'Come in Hana!' I say again, and she opens her eyes and reluctantly picks up her sandals and walks back into the courtyard.

'I'm hungry!'

'Well, you shouldn't have been outside when the breakfast was cooked. Daanish will be here in a moment; there is no time now.'

'Mama! No! I am hungry!'

And I smile 'It is okay, I was only joking. There is plenty of time, but come and eat now or it will be cold.'

'Okay, Mama,' she says. 'Mama, what has happened to Naira's face? It looks as though she has been eaten by crocodiles.'

I pause in what I am doing for a moment, and then I say 'She was very upset two days ago, but she is alright now. It is best not to talk about it.'

I say this in a way that is intended to discourage her from mentioning it again, but she looks doubtfully at me and says 'Mama?'

'Hurry up and eat your breakfast, or you will be going without!' I say quickly, and then go out into the yard to see if Maajid would like any more chai before he goes to work.

Maajid is reading yesterday's newspaper as well as listening to the radio. Yesterday, he did not rise from his bed, but slept for a large part of the day. He did not want to eat until it was time for supper, when I brought his in to him, and then we both ate together in our room and in the end he had a good appetite. Afterwards, he fell asleep again almost immediately, and was awake before me at dawn. Today, he seems to be back to his old self. 'Tariq, you may come with me into Kannapur,' he says. 'Did you hear what they have done? They have blown up the railway line, again. I hope that you did not have any plans to catch a train anytime soon. How could they guard all of the line?' he ponders. 'There are thousands of miles of it in India. If the bandits want to blow it up I don't see how anyone can stop them. Why do they do it, though? In the newspaper it says they believe that they are fighting for the people, well, if they blow up the railway lines then how are the people to go about their business, eh? Tell me that.'

'I don't know,' says Tariq. 'They are crazy. It is because there are to be elections, I think. They always do things like that before an election. They will probably start shooting people again, soon. They always do that, too.'

'Doesn't your boss use the railway?' asks Maajid.

'Sometimes he does. Sometimes he gets an auto.'

'What, even if he goes all the way to Patna?'

'Yes, sometimes. It isn't as crowded as the train or the bus.'

Maajid shrugs in a way that suggests that Tariq's boss must be crazy to do such a thing and then he stands up and folds the newspaper slowly, deliberately, and carefully into a shape that will slip into his back pocket and says 'Come on, then' and goes to start up the motorbike.

They ride out of the gateway as Daanish arrives, and it really does seem sometimes that he must almost wait for Maajid and Tariq to go before he arrives at the gate, so often do the two events coincide in that way. Then the girls run out and squeeze into the back and I say 'Goodbye, have a good day at school,' and they wave back and say 'Goodbye Mama,' and the other little girls smile and wave at me too, and I turn and go back into the courtyard and close the gate and return to the kitchen to speak to Naira about what we need to do today.

The overnight cold has taken an old man in his wooden stall. Tanu lived next to the village chai stall, and supplied much of the village with their treats and essentials. After he had opened up his stall each day, he would hang up displays of chips and biscuits and strips of gum and packets of fried dal, and in the glass fronted cabinet there would be soaps and plasters, cigarettes and gum, all sorts of packets of sweets and lollies and razor blades and matches, and there would be one or two sacks on the floor of potatoes or onions, and everything else would be on shelves around him. Tanu sat all day cross-legged on a metal chair behind his wooden desk which stood behind the glass fronted cabinet, serving and chatting and grinning with a huge gap- and brown-toothed grin. He wore old-fashioned spectacles like the ones that Gandhi is pictured as wearing, only Tanu's were mended in several places with tape and one of the lenses had a crack across the very middle. His stall is made from rough planks of wood attached to a frame of palm trunks, and the roof is of palm fronds piled and spread thickly on top of the frame. The wall on the other side from the chai stall is lined with pieces of plastic to keep out wind and rain. Other than his chair, his cabinet and his desk, Tanu's only possessions were a few pans, his clothes, his charpoy and a brown woollen blanket.

At lunchtime, Tanu would be brought a metal plate from the chai stall with rice and dal and vegetables. He would take a ten rupee note from his drawer and hand it over, then sit and eat his meal and then put the plate down on the ground beside the cabinet where it stayed until the owner of the chai stall brought Tanu a glass of sweet tea and took the plate away again. Later, when the sun disappeared behind the houses opposite, Tanu would take down his displays of chips and biscuits and strips of gum and packets of fried dal, and pull a screen of woven palm leaves across the front of his stall and no one would see him again until the morning.

Then he would pull the screen of palm leaves away again and lean it against the side of his stall, and perform a simple puja on the earth beside the roadway; placing a small bowl of water on the ground and burning a single incense stick before it, while praying quietly to his god.

Today the glass fronted cabinet still has its stock of treats and essentials, but Tanu did not awake this morning. When the owner of the tea stall arrived to open up and saw that the old man was not about, he called him and when he received no answer, he moved the screen and went into the stall. Behind the shelves that stood behind Tanu's metal chair, the old man lay on his charpoy, one bony leg protruding out from underneath the blanket which was pulled up beneath his chin, as if he were still fast asleep. But his blanket was no longer able to keep him warm, and he had ceased to feel the cold. Now the screen is back across the front of his stall, and the old man's eldest son has been summoned from Kannapur to arrange his funeral and decide what is to happen to the stall. In the tea stall, the men sip chai and speak quietly of Tanu and nod occasionally in the direction of his body.

Naira received this news from one of her friends at the gate just after breakfast when she went out for water, and after that she went out to buy the food that we will need today. Her way to the couple of little stalls that make up the village market takes her past Tanu's stall and the chai stall, and she slows down and stops to speak to one of the women who are standing nearby. They are talking and looking at the closed stall, and she hears more of what has happened. She shakes her head with the others, and says 'Who will have the stall now?'

One of the other women says 'Maybe his youngest son, because I don't think the others would be interested; they have shops in Kannapur and who would give up a shop in Kannapur to have this little stall here? It is not much of a living, and when the rains come it is no good. You have to close it up, because the rain gets in no matter what you do, and ruins the goods.' Tanu used to go to stay with his eldest son then, because their shops and houses are of concrete. When he came back everything had to be dried out before it could be used, and he had to bring back all of the stock that he had taken to Kannapur.

'And you cannot lock it up,' another woman adds. 'Whoever has it will have to live there, or everything would be stolen overnight. And it is too small for more than a couple; they could not have children there.'

'You would know if they were trying to make some, though,' says the first with a laugh, as the walls might as well not be there they are so flimsy and full of holes.

Tanu's son is standing in front of his father's stall and stroking his chin, holding a glass of chai and talking quietly to the chai stall owner. He has already walked around the back of the stall, where the ground slopes down to the river and the old man grew a few onions and a bit of spinach that he rarely ate himself. Everyone knew that the chai stall owner helped himself to them now and again. They glance occasionally at the knot of women chattering beside them, finally moving a couple of steps away so as not to be overheard, or possibly so that they can hear themselves speak.

I was glad to see Naira walk out of the gates, for at the moment every time that I see her face, I feel as though it is a reproach. I am certain that everybody must blame me for her injuries. Naira defends me, naturally, but her denials seem to me so half-hearted that I think everybody takes them to actually be an accusation of me. I do not know what she has said to Tariq.

And, in a way, I think, I am responsible. But then I think about it some more, as I have been for these last two days. I have been thinking about the strange loss of my jewellery and its even stranger discovery in the latrine, and trying to understand what it might mean. I do not doubt that if a robber got into the house, then he must have come through the gateway that Naira had left open, because it clearly could not have been through one of the windows as there are bars on all of them. They must have walked into the yard and then in through the doorway and opened the trunk, perhaps in a hurry, as they spilled everything out and overturned it and broke the hinge, and I wonder why it was only my trunk in our room that they opened. Nothing else had been disturbed in there, nothing in the girls' room, and if there was anything in Tariq and Naira's room, then nothing was said which would seem very strange if that was the case, and so I assume that there was not.

If a robber did get into our house, then, I wonder why it was that they went straight into our room, and straight to where my jewellery was kept. It is almost as if they knew that it was the place that they would find it. And I wonder again how it was that they were not seen, because if the gate was open, then it can be seen by anyone at the pump. Naira or anyone else would only have to look up at the right time, to see them going in or coming out. Everyone in the village would know that. There were no strangers in the village, either, because they would have been noticed and talked about and we would have heard, and even if there was, let us say that a stranger took a chance and did sneak in through the gate, did ransack our room and find my jewellery and go out into the yard, then why would he have left it in the latrine and not just run off with it?

If a robber did get into the house, of course.

I wonder if the important part of this strange puzzle is that it was Naira who found the jewellery. I wonder if that was the whole purpose of it. I feel that Naira is very fragile at the moment and she frightens me a little. I was most surprised that she immediately confessed to having left the gate open, and I wonder if that might have been to draw attention to the fact. I remember my thinking that her surprise when she came into our room sounded false to my ears. I wonder whether she took the jewellery herself with the intention of finding it and restoring it to me so as to earn my thanks and my praise. It is true that she is my daughter in law, and that we do not get on very well, but that is the way that it always is, and no one expects it to be any different. For the moment, though, I do not think that I will say anything of this to her. I do not think that I will say anything to Maajid, either, because I do not think that he will agree that it is likely, but if he did then I think that he would be furious with Naira, which would not help anyone. So I will hold my tongue for now. But, oh Naira! There was a madness in your eyes!

There is another thing that is worrying me, and I do not know why. For some reason I have been thinking again about the dog we had that died a week ago. There was a rat in the yard yesterday morning, which made Naira scream a little because it surprised her, and almost ran across her foot as she was coming out of the kitchen, and she said 'Oh no! We must get another dog if there are rats here, because we don't want those in the kitchen!' Naturally, I said 'No, we don't. Perhaps we must get another,' but then I found myself thinking about the dog again, and wondering why I did.

FIVE

In my dream I am sad. I am sad because there is a horrible void inside of me.

I am young. I have been a wife for no more than three years, and already we have a son. My mother in law has become a little kinder since Tariq was born, and it is a year since she last raised her hand to me. Tariq is now walking, and is being spoilt each day by his proud grandparents.

We have had another child, but this one did not survive.

'I do not understand why you are so upset,' Maajid says to me, irritably. 'It was only a girl.' But there is something in his eyes that tells me he feels otherwise. It is what his parents want to hear; it is not really for my ears, it is for them. And I am furious with him because our baby has died and he is not really speaking to me. We are all sitting in the courtyard in the afternoon sun. I have been crying, and now I need to sleep. Amma is drinking a cup of chai, and is sitting with her back to me. And she does not look at me as she speaks.

'It is a relief,' Is all she says.

In my dream I am sad, because I know that this will happen again and again, and that for almost ten years we fear that we shall have no more children. And then within the space of a year and a half, our precious little girls are born. It has been so long since a tiny voice called me Mama!

'Mama! Mama!' It takes me a moment or two to realize that I am not dreaming, and then I look at the time and see that it is almost half past one in the morning.

'What is the matter, Leila?'

'Hana has a pain, Mama. Can you give her something?' I sit up now, suddenly wide awake.

'I'm just coming.' I hear her leave the room, and then almost immediately she is back again.

'Mama! She has been sick!'

'Alright'. I fumble around to find the lamp and the matches, and once it is lit I go out onto the veranda and into the girls' room. Hana is lying on her side, on the ground beside her bedroll, crying and clutching her stomach. 'Oh, my poor little girl!' I put the lamp on their trunk and get down onto my knees beside Hana. 'Where is the pain, little one? In your stomach?'

'Yes, Mama,' she manages to say, through her tears. 'It is horrible!' I put my hand to her forehead, and she feels very clammy; although she is sweating, her skin is unpleasantly cool to my touch. She has been sick on her bedroll and on her blanket and it is over her clothes.

'Can you sit up, Hana?' She makes an attempt to do so, but her face creases and her sobs become louder, and almost immediately she gives up the effort and collapses back onto her side again.

'No...I can't, Mama! I'm sorry!'

'It's alright.' I stroke her head for a moment and then I hear a sound and look around to see Naira standing in the doorway.

'I heard noises. What is the matter?'

'Hana has a bad stomach, now. The poor girl has been sick.'

'Oh,' she makes a tutting noise. 'You stay here with her, Amma, I'll make her something.'

'Oh, thank you, Naira,' I say, but she has gone. Immediately, Hana's crying grows louder and more urgent and she turns her head to be sick again. 'Oh, Hana! Come, I'll sit you up.' I hoist her up and help her take off her messy clothing and put it on the floor with the blanket, then lean her against me and put my arms around her. Leila has come over to kneel beside us, and now she is crying too.

'Oh, Mama! Is Hana going to be alright?'

'Of course she is, Leila. She just has an upset stomach. It was probably sucking on that dirty ice, yesterday. Do you feel alright?'

Yes, Mama.'

'That is good, anyway. Hana, do you feel any better, yet?'

'No, Mama. I still feel sick. Oh, Mama!' she begins to wail. 'Am I going to die?'

'Of course you're not, you silly girl! You just have an upset stomach. Naira has gone to make you up something to drink to make you feel better. Then I'll sort out your bed and you can lie down again and try to get some sleep. Her sobs slowly subside and I think that she is getting sleepier and feel my own eyes beginning to close as well, when there is a light in the doorway and Naira reappears. She is holding a mug.

'Here, Hana, I have made you a drink,' she says, softly. 'Full of good things to help your stomach feel better.' I am fully awake again, and I gently lift Hana more upright.

'Oh, thank you, Naira. That was quick,' I say.

'Thank you, Naira,' Hana echoes. Naira beams with pleasure and hands me the mug.

'I will get you some more when you have drunk this.' I hold the mug to Hana's mouth and she puts her hands over mine and tips it and begins to sip. I smell the comforting scents of the herbs rising up between our faces and smile at Hana, who does not notice, but smiles slightly anyway.

'This is nice. I could drink this all the time, Mama!'

'It is only for when you are not well.' I sense rather than hear Naira leaving the room, and then she is back almost immediately with a bucket which she puts down on the floor and comes forward and squats down beside us.

'Let me take the bedroll and blanket and I'll wash them in the morning. I can find another blanket and something for Hana to sleep on. Then give me her soiled clothes and I'll wash them too.' She gathers them up and leaves the room, returning a few minutes later with a blanket and another bedroll which she puts down near the door, before bringing over the bucket which I now see contains warm water, steaming slightly in the lamplight, and a rag. 'I have put some soap in,' she says, wiping the floor around us.

'Where did you find the bedroll?' I ask. 'I was going to bring in a charpoy from the veranda.'

'Oh, it is mine,' she replies. 'It does not matter for one night.'

'Oh, no, Naira!' I protest. 'You do not need to do that. Hana will be fine on a charpoy, won't you Hana?'

'Of course, Mama.'

'She'll be too cold, at this time of year,' says Naira, firmly. 'Let her sleep on mine. It is only for one night.' She finishes wiping the floor and bustles out of the room, bucket in hand. A few minutes later she is back.

'Would you like some more of the drink, Hana?'

'Yes, please,' she replies, handing Naira the mug.

'How are you feeling now, little one?' I ask her, as Naira leaves the room.

'Maybe a *little* better, Mama. I think that the drink has helped.'

'That is good.' She leans her head against me again.

'I do not feel so sick, now.'

'Good. Maybe when you have had the other mug you could try to lie down again.'

'Alright, Mama.' And now Naira is back and handing Hana the drink.

'I'll go and move the charpoy now, and I'll wash the clothes first thing in the morning after breakfast. Goodnight, call me if you need to.'

I don't answer, because again something is making me feel a little uneasy. That was quick, I had said to Naira, and now I ponder this. It was really very, *very* quick.

SIX

This morning, the birds seem to be singing louder than usual, and I wonder why that might be or whether, of course, I am simply imagining it to be so. There is no ice this morning; there has been a slight breeze for much of the night, and it is warmer than it was at dawn yesterday. Behind the house, the sun appears and disappears behind low, slowly moving dark clouds that appear silvery around the edges, and there is a pale haze around the sun each time that it does appear.

Hana seemed to sleep well after she laid down again last night, neither waking her sister nor anyone else in the house. I got up a little before dawn and crept into the girls' room and stood by the doorway, listening to the even sounds of breathing coming from my daughters, and felt reassured. I wanted to creep forward and bend down and kiss them both, to hold them in my arms as they slept, but I was fearful, especially, of waking Hana. Instead, after a while I crept out of the room again, and returned to my own bed where I lay sleeplessly for another half an hour or so, until I determined that it was time for me to get up.

When I went into the kitchen, the fire was still warm, and so it was the work of just a few moments to build it up and go to the pump. Soon there was water on, and I had put out the mugs, and then the chai was boiling, and so I went outside to stand in the yard, looking up at the sky and thinking my thoughts until the chai should be ready. Then I would go and see whether Leila was awake, and how Hana was; whether she was still sleeping or whether she lay there talking and giggling with her sister as they often did in the mornings, instead of getting up when they should.

Naira comes out into the yard and says 'How is Hana this morning?'

'She was still sleeping a little while ago, and I was about to go and see.'

'You go. Is the chai on?'

'Yes, and the mugs are out, so pour it out if I am not back.'

I turn and go up onto the veranda, and at the doorway to the girls' room I stop and look inside, and see Leila sitting on the floor in her school uniform combing her hair. Hana is sleeping beside her, and as I look Leila turns around and puts her fingers to her lips. I smile and walk softly into the room.

'Are you alright this morning, Leila?' and I give her a kiss.

'Yes, Mama. Hana is still sleeping.'

'That is good. Leave her.' I bend down and feel Hana's forehead, but I am slightly worried because she still feels a little feverish and I wonder whether I ought to wake her and give her another drink, but then think no, she has not been sick again, and the sleep will be good for her, and so I go back outside again.

'How is my little girl this morning?' asks Maajid, when he comes out.

'She is alright. She is still sleeping, and I will keep her at home today so that she can have a good sleep, and hopefully she will then feel better and be able to go back to school tomorrow.'

'Isn't it Sunday tomorrow?'

'Oh, of course it is. I am tired. Well she will have two days off then. I am sure that she will not mind that. Have you seen her?'

'No.'

'Well go in and see her then, only don't wake her if she is still asleep.'

'Alright,' he says and goes off to look in on Hana. When I come out of the kitchen next he is sitting on his chair in the yard and he has switched on the radio and is trying to tune it.

'Who has been fiddling with this?' He asks, although he does not look at me as he says it, and I don't think he really expects an answer.

'I don't know,' I say, anyway. 'Was Hana still sleeping?'

'Yes,' he says. 'Ah, got it.' He puts the radio down beneath the chair. 'She feels hot.'

'Do you think so? I thought she felt clammy.'

'Well she feels like she has a bit of a fever anyway.'

'Yes, that's what I thought. I will see how she is later.'

'It is strange that she should have a bad stomach like that so soon after I did.'

'Yes, it is strange,' I say.

'I will get my sister a little something,' says Tariq, 'when I am in the town. Perhaps a bangle or something.'

'You did not get anything for your poor father when he was ill!' laughs Maajid. 'Are you ready?'

'Where is Leila?' I ask. 'Is she ready?'

'I don't know. See you later.'

'Leila? Where are you? Hurry up!'

'There is something I must tell you,' says Naira, but now I am suddenly feeling flustered and irritated.

'Can it wait for a moment? I need to find a coin for Leila, as Daanish will be here any time now. Tell me after that.'

'Alright,' she says.

But when everyone has gone, she seems in no hurry to say what was on her mind, and I don't remind her. So we do the shopping list, and I say 'Do you want to go or shall I?'

'You go, today, if you like.' So I take the basket and go out of the yard, and pull the gate across, and walk off towards the market, wondering whether I should have asked her what she was going to say.

Tanu's body has been taken to the cremation ground in Kannapur, and the screen is across the front of the stall again. He will be cremated later today, and the chai stall owner will be there, as he was counted one of Tanu's friends and had known him for many years, so his son is at the stall to look after it for the day. As I pass by, the owner is giving him some last minute advice, and going by the laughter amongst the chai drinkers sitting on the benches, he is also getting some advice from them as well. He looks a little unsure of himself, as if he does not know whether he is having his leg pulled or not.

When I get back to the house Naira has swept outside the gate and along beside the wall, she has thrown water on the ground to dampen down the dust and is now sweeping the yard. 'I have done the breakfast things,' she says, 'and Hana is still sleeping, although she woke up just after you had gone out and wanted a drink. I gave her some boiled water, but she does not want anything to eat at the moment. I will go and wash her clothing when I am done here.'

She looks triumphantly at me, and I decide that, in a way, I preferred the old Naira, who would have been finding a reason to do as little as possible. But then I feel guilty for thinking that; maybe she is just trying her hardest to be one of the family. I suppose I should be grateful for that, and encourage her, so I say 'Thank you. Would you like some chai, Naira?'

And she says 'Yes, I will just finish sweeping here, and then I will get some water.'

'Oh, that's alright,' I say. 'I'll get it.' and I take a pot from the kitchen and go across the road to the pump.

I do that, and I go into the kitchen and put another dung cake onto the fire, waiting while the flames grow and it begins to burn, and then I place the pot over the fire and look for the mugs. When I go outside again, Naira is coming out of the girls' room and smiling, and she says 'Hana is awake now, and I wonder whether she would like something to eat.'

'Did you ask her?' I say.

'No, but I think that it would do her good.'

And so I go in to see Hana, and say 'Hello, little one. Are you feeling any better, now?'

'A little, Mama,' she says. 'I don't want to get up, though. I am very sleepy.'

'Would you like anything to eat?'

'Oh, no, Mama, I couldn't. I think I would be sick again!'

'Let me feel your head,' I say. 'It feels better, now. That's good. I don't think we'll have to take you to the hospital, yet.'

'Oh, Mama! You wouldn't, would you?'

'No, of course not. You're much better, now. Naira thinks you should have something to eat'. Hana makes a face.

'No, Mama!'

'It's alright, Hana. If she brings it, say you will have it later, and leave it beside you on the floor.'

Naira has a dish with some cold meat and rice, and is hovering just outside the doorway when I come out, so I say 'Oh, thank you, Naira. That is kind.' I stand aside so that she can go past, and then in turn I hover outside and hear Naira encouraging Hana to eat, and Hana saying 'Thank you, if you put it down there I will try to eat some a bit later.'

Then Naira comes out again and says 'I will clean their room a little later. I am sure she will feel better if I do that.' And then we go to get the chai, and we sit down in the sunshine in the courtyard for a few minutes without speaking while we drink the chai, and I think should I ask her now what she wanted to say? But then I think no, it's probably better if she tells me whatever it is when she is ready. But there is a tension in the air again, and I am not sure if it is my imagination or not.

Now I feel that I need to think quietly, because she is beginning to irritate me once more just with her presence, and I am fearful of saying the wrong thing and offending her deeply. I feel a little frightened still of the side of her that I saw recently, although it is surely not right that I should be in awe of my son's wife, and so I say 'Why don't you go and see your parents this afternoon? I think it is a long time since you last went, and I am sure that they would be pleased to see you. When we have done everything that we need to do, other than prepare supper, and I will do that, then you could go over there. You can come back by supper then can't you?'

She smiles and puts her mug down on the ground and says 'Thank you, I will do that,' and I sense that she will be glad to get away from here for a while, too.

Then later it is the afternoon, and she has gone. I am in the kitchen working, and Leila has just returned from school. She is sitting on the veranda doing her homework, and Hana has got up and is sitting close beside her sister with a blanket around her shoulders, leaning against the wall of the house. I think to myself that tomorrow we will go back to normal and I will treat Naira the same as I did before, only slightly more gently, I quickly remind myself, and I will not be afraid of her new moods. I will ask her what it was that she wanted to say to me, and so I will prove to myself that she does not frighten me.

Another couple of hours later, I am in the kitchen again. I am cooking supper when I hear the sound of the motorbike coming down the road, and then I hear it stop at the gate. There are voices, briefly, shouting above the sound of the engine, the gate scrapes open, the bike revs up its engine again, and it roars into the yard, or at least so it sounds to me, as it is so much louder, then the engine cuts out and it is quiet again, other than for the voices and the gate scraping shut. Now Tariq and Maajid are at the doorway, and calling out for Hana.

'Where is she?' asks Tariq. 'Is she feeling any better? I have a little something for my poor sickly sister. I don't suppose that it will make her feel any better, but I hope that she will like it anyway.'

'I am sure she will like it,' says Maajid. 'She is very fond of her big brother, and it will please her that he has been thinking of her.'

Hana walks slowly into the kitchen with her blanket around her shoulders and says 'Hello Baba, hello Tariq.'

'Are you feeling better, now?' asks Tariq, holding up a silver bracelet. 'I thought you might like this, little sister.'

'Oh, that's lovely!' says Hana, brightening up immediately. 'Can I try it on?' She slips it over her hand and admires it on her wrist.

'It looks very nice on you,' smiles Maajid. 'I can see you're feeling better now.'

'Well, not *completely* better,' says Hana coyly, obviously enjoying being the centre of all this attention, 'but I *am* better than I was this morning. Can I have some supper tonight, Mama?'

'Of course you can, Hana.'

'Where is Naira, Mother?' Asks Tariq.

'Oh, she is not back yet. She went over to see her parents this afternoon.'

'Her parents?'

'Yes, I thought it would be nice for her. I don't think that she has seen them for a while, and we had done everything that needed to be done.'

'But it is almost dark now.'

'Yes, I am sure she will be back any minute. She will see that it is getting dark.' But now I am slightly worried, too. It is getting dark and no woman should be out on her own then.

'Why don't you take the motorbike and go to meet her?' says Maajid.

'Yes, I think perhaps I will, says Tariq. 'Give me the key, thank you.' But before he can even walk out into the yard, there is a sudden hammering on the gates, and we look at each other, but Tariq strides out quickly and pulls open the gates. Naira is outside, and she is shaking and crying and leaning with her arm against the gatepost, and unable to speak. We all tumble out of the doorway and stand behind Tariq, and no one speaks or even moves for a long moment. We are all looking at her and thinking...what are we thinking? I am thinking something awful has happened, and it was me who suggested to her that she go to her parents this afternoon, and so it is all my fault again. And I cannot speak, and it seems that no one can speak; who is going to speak? Somebody speak! my brain screams out, and in the end it is Leila who speaks, who I hadn't even noticed was there and she says 'Naira? What has happened?'

And at that everyone is suddenly speaking.

'What has happened?' echoes Maajid, and:

'Naira! Tell me what has happened!' demands Tariq, and I hear Hana speak, but I cannot hear what she says, and I say 'Naira?' weakly and Leila has begun to cry because she knows that it is something bad although she does not know what it is and does not understand the fears of the adults. And Naira still does not say anything, but looks from one of us to another to another as if searching on our faces for a sign of some sort, and then she lets go of the gatepost and takes a step forward towards Tariq, and whispers his name but he takes a step backwards and says 'What is this? What are you going to tell me?' And she replies 'Please, Tariq!'

'You are going to tell me you have been with a man!' he shouts, and his face is suddenly furious and hateful and he does not look like Tariq who is my son.

'No!' says Naira, 'At least I didn't do anything; there was a man on the way home, and he was following me.'

'You must have done something to make him do that!'

'No, I didn't! Please, you must believe me!' And she lifts her head and takes a deep breath and says 'Tariq! I...'

But he will not let her speak and shouts again 'What has happened then that is so bad, if you say it is not what I think it is?' Then he grabs her arm and pulls her towards him and she cries out in pain and now I can see in her eyes that she is scared of Tariq and I do not know if she has seen him like this before but I have not and I do not want the girls to see it either and I tell them 'Quickly, now, go to your room!' and I see that they, too, are scared but I shoo them across the yard and see them disappear through their doorway, and then I turn around and go back to the gateway in time to see Maajid close the gate, so that no one outside will be able to see what is going on and Naira is saying 'No, I didn't' but Tariq slaps her across the face and says 'Liar!'

'Tariq! No!' I begin to say, but 'Be quiet, woman!' shouts Maajid 'She is his wife!'

'I should throw you out of our house,' Tariq continues 'if you have done anything with another man! Go to our room, now! I do not wish to do all this in front of my family.' Naira lowers her head and walks across the yard to their room and Tariq follows after her. At the doorway she looks back towards us for a moment, but then pulls aside the curtain and they both go in.

Maajid simply looks at me and says 'I'm hungry, Siddiqa. What is for supper?'

SEVEN

The four of us eat supper on the veranda just outside
the kitchen, in the light of a kerosene lamp that hangs
from a nail in the post nearest to us and swings gently in
the rising breeze. Our shadows hover around us and
dart backwards and forwards, while the candle that I
can see through the kitchen doorway flickers and
gutters. The room and the courtyard are filled with
threatening presences. There are clouds in the sky that
hide the moon and the stars, so that we sit in an
uncertain oasis of light, while the unseen world outside
sniffs around the edges.

We are jumpy and irritable with each other, which
is not helped by the occasional shouts and the sounds
of slowly moving vehicles somewhere beyond our walls.
There has been low speech from Tariq and Naira's room
that I have tried not to listen to, but would really like to
hear. I cannot make it out, though. There was a cry at
one point, and I almost jumped to my feet, but it has
not been repeated and now all is silence from that
corner of the house. I do not know whether everything

has been resolved, or whether everything is dreadful and miserable.

'I will clean the dishes, Mama.' says Leila, breaking the silence that has become terrible, but I say 'No, leave them until the morning.' I do not want the gate to be opened again tonight, as I am fearful of something that I cannot name, but which lurks outside. I know that it has already found its way into our house, but I still have to try to keep it out, and I know of no other way than to keep the gate closed and to rely on the bars on the window, and on my vigilance.

I am frightened for my daughters.

As I send them to bed, there is a flash of lightning in the distance, although there is no thunder yet, and no rain. I gather together the dishes, and pile them in the corner of the yard away from the kitchen, so that mice and rats will not be attracted there. Then I put a small pot of water over the fire to boil, so that Maajid and I might have chai before we go to bed, and I put the pans with the rice and the vegetables on the highest shelf in the kitchen, with lids covering them, in case Tariq or Naira might decide that they want some supper later.

There are a few spots of rain falling, but there has been no more lightning yet, and I stand for a while just by the edge of the veranda, in case it should suddenly pour down. At the moment, though, there are just these few drops of rain, but they are big drops, and I know that there is a storm coming at some time during the night. But for now I stand still, and I feel the drops on my head, and on my upturned face, as I look up into the dark and see nothing but blackness. And the raindrops that land on my face have fallen a long, long way through the invisible sky, perhaps for miles, and why is it that I feel a curious jealousy of the rain and the clouds and the wind?

My home was in a different village to this one, over five miles away. It is a while since I have thought of my old home, but now, on the very edge of sleep, it suddenly comes into my mind. Perhaps my thoughts have led me here without my realizing it. I had been thinking that if I had not told Naira to visit her parents today, then none of the bad things after that would have happened. Then maybe I had thought that my mother in law had never let me do that, and how I wished that she had, and that I would now, suddenly, really like to go to see them, and not noticed those thoughts; if you can have thoughts without noticing them, that is. I suppose that you can, because it is easy to be thinking about things and then to suddenly completely forget what it was that you were thinking about, which is what I think that I have done now.

I miss my brother, too. Like Hana and Leila, I had one brother who was older than me, although not so old as Tariq is to his sisters. He was married just before me, and he brought his new wife to live at home a few months before I was married. Tamim was my constant companion until he was almost old enough to marry, and was kind and strong and gentle, and even spent a lot of his time teaching me his school lessons, since girls were not often sent to school, then, at least not in our village. When I think of him, I see him as a sixteen year old youth, but he now has grandchildren and I have no photograph of him, either, and I have yet to see those grandchildren, although I have met all of his children at one time or another, and have photographs of some of them.

But after I was married, I hardly ever saw him again, for it is not right that a wife should spend time at her old home. It is no longer her home, and would that I had remembered that myself today! But I could not have walked to my parents' house to visit them and come back without taking the whole of the day, in any case, which would have been out of the question. We had no transport in the village then, except for a few bicycles and carts and, I think, a couple of motorbikes, although no one in our family had one. It is much easier to go to the other villages or into the town now, for everyone seems to have some sort of transport and, of course, Naira does not need to worry about that, because her parents are living just a quarter of an hour away on the other side of the village. This means, of course, that she can easily visit them when she should be doing the shopping, although I should not be thinking that just at this moment, and now I feel bad for having done so.

I do not yet know any more about what did happen today – yesterday, I mean, as it is now gone midnight – since we did not see either Tariq or Naira again in the evening. Although their room is next to ours, I have not heard any sounds, either, since we have come to bed. They might have crept out of the house and disappeared, for all that I can tell. And now, in the darkness of the night, and with the distant rumbling of the thunderstorm still sounding occasionally, I even begin to wonder whether they might have done so, although I know that these fears are foolish and stupid. The thunderstorm finally broke about an hour ago; there was a flash of lightning, and almost instantly a crash of thunder that made me jump and woke Maajid. *'What's that?'* 'It's thunder.' *'Oh, it sounded like an explosion. Are you alright?'* 'Me?' *'Yes.'* I was surprised at that. 'I'm alright. I was already awake. Go back to sleep.' And then the rain was drumming on the roof, almost as loud as the thunder itself.

When it does rain, it always sounds loud, for our house is roofed with corrugated metal sheets. The first few drops were big and musical, sounding rather like drumbeats, but on different instruments, as each one sounded very slightly different to the others. But then they multiplied rapidly over and over again, and the sound of the rain became almost like a long, continuous roll of thunder and sleep was impossible. We both lay there awake, but neither of us spoke, for if sleep was impossible, then so, too, was conversation, for it would have been necessary to shout to be able to make oneself heard above the din of the rainstorm. It was so loud, that it was almost impossible to hear the regular peals of thunder, and it was only the lightning flashes that told me that it had not stopped.

And then there was less than a slight breeze; a movement in the air around my face, and I jumped slightly, as two small girls were suddenly lying either side of me, their arms snaked around me, and a face buried into my neck on each side. I just heard 'Mama, I'm scared!' and now I could feel Maajid's arms, too, and feel him shaking, and I knew that he was laughing. But we all lay together as the rain and the thunder reached its peak, and I suddenly wanted to cry. But this time it was because I felt happy at that moment, and I wanted it to last forever, and I knew that it wouldn't. I knew that it never would.

And now the girls have returned to their own beds in their own room, and Maajid is asleep again. When the girls finally got to their feet and went out, and the curtain swished shut behind them, I lay for some while looking into the darkness in Maajid's direction, wondering whether he was still awake. I was wishing that he might reach out to me, because I had just been happy, and he had been jovial and tender, and I wanted him to reach out to me and it would have been a good time for him to do that, but then he began to snore and I lay still feeling suddenly numb again.

It has become colder; the rain has brought a chill to the night air that had not been there before. Although I am shivering, I have got up from my blankets and I have walked outside and I am sitting on the edge of the veranda in the dark. I have my shawl around my shoulders, and the sounds of the night all around me. Always, there seem to be the sounds of the crickets. Every now and again a dog barks, and I am waiting for the fox to come along the street, but, since I am waiting for him, he will probably decide not to come into the village tonight, unless I have missed him, of course. It is too late for there to be any traffic. Even the young ones who keep late nights have made their way back to their homes, now, and I feel that I am the only person awake in the entire village. I can hear Maajid snoring gently, and I strain my ears to listen for sounds from Tariq and Naira's room, but I do not think that I can hear anything. They are both young, and the young do not seem to snore the way that we do as we get older. I pray that there has been no violence.

I cannot sleep, tonight. I fear that there has been violence.

There are puddles in the yard; I am dipping the big toe of my right foot into the edge of one, and I am swirling the water round and around, although I can hardly see this water. Even though my eyes have adjusted to the darkness, there are very few stars to be seen in the sky, as there are many clouds still moving overhead. I swirl the water round and when I tire of this, I feel the mud with my toes and I begin to rub my foot gently in the mud. It feels very nice, and now my whole foot is in the mud; not just the toes, but the heel also, and now I put the other foot in beside it, and thoughtfully I sit sliding my feet slowly around in this mud.

I am getting cold, now, but I am still afraid. I am afraid of what might have happened. I want the night to be over and morning to come so that I can find out what has happened.

I want to go to sleep and dream my harmless dreams, and wake up when the dawn light is in the sky, but although I am tired I do not think that I will be able to sleep. Eventually, though, I am feeling so tired that I get up and creep into the room and wipe my feet and lie down and I go to sleep.

EIGHT

When I get up in the morning, Naira is bringing the water in from the pump as though nothing unusual has happened. She glances at me, and she smiles gently, but the smile does not touch any part of her face except her mouth. And as she passes me I see that she has a bruise on her cheek, just below her left eye. It is raw and dark, and the skin has split apart enough for it to have bled a little. Her upper lip also looks to be swollen, even in that half-light that fills the yard before the sun has risen.

'Salaam, Naira,' I say hesitantly, immediately unsure of why I am a little fearful of speaking to her. I cannot imagine that Tariq would seek to forbid me, and since we have much to do in the house together that would be impossible in any case. Perhaps I am just afraid of saying the wrong thing; I fear that even innocent words may sometimes cause harm.

I am relieved, at least, to find that Naira is still in the house, for there was a part of me that thought that Tariq might have pushed her out of the gate last night, and told her to go back to her parents.

But for the moment, there is to be no conversation anyway, for Naira does not stop. She merely pulls the gate closed behind her, and goes into the kitchen. But as she passes me, I have the feeling that she is trying very hard not to cry, and it suddenly makes me want to weep as well. For what seems to be a long time, I stand there watching her as she goes through the doorway into the kitchen and then begins to set the fire, and I do not know what to say or do.

Eventually, I use the latrine, and take my toothbrush and go out to the pump. A neighbour is already there brushing her teeth, and I nod and smile at her. But in return she looks at me with hard eyes, and rinses her mouth, and spits with more force than is necessary. Then she wipes her face with the cloth that she has brought out with her, and leaves without speaking to me. I know that Naira is friendly with her, and I feel that everyone, the whole world, is blaming me for Naira's injuries, and I want to run after her and grab her by the shoulder and say Stop! Listen to me! I did not do any of that! It is not my fault! But I don't, and I wonder whether it is because I cannot help feeling that it is, really, my fault, although I never meant Naira any harm.

But I know, also, that you do not need to mean someone any harm to do them an injury. It is like an accident, or something unexpected that gets out of control. It is like the buffalo that steps out in front of the unwary motorbike rider and causes him to fall from his bike – the buffalo does not mean the rider any harm, yet the accident happens anyway. The rider is injured, and it is not really anyone's fault, except maybe for the rider, if he was driving too fast or not paying proper attention to what he was doing, but other than that no one had the intention to harm him. Unless you agree that it was fate, that it was his fate. The Hindus would say it was his karma, and that he had caused it to happen to himself in some other life, when he did the creature that is now the buffalo a wrong. Or it might be that it is fate, and that God had decreed that he should be killed or injured that way, as that was the purpose that he had in mind for him. Or perhaps he was being punished for his bad deeds, and maybe he had been blasphemous or had broken one of the tenets of the Koran. We cannot otherwise hope to understand why this accident should happen, and the Moslems would say that. Thus all are agreed that it was his fate, and so it must have been Naira's fate to suffer as she is at the moment.

But now the woman has gone, and so I go back through the gateway into the yard. I put my toothbrush away, and go into the kitchen to see that Naira has the fire alight and the pot of water already on top of the cooker. Wordlessly, I put out the mugs and I get the tea, the milk, the spices and the sugar, and then I turn towards Naira. But she does not seem to want to look at me, and so I look away again and I wonder what I can say to break the silence.

Everything is different today. I feel as though we are going to have to find a new way of speaking to each other, but I do not know whether Naira wishes to speak, or if she would rather work in silence today and just think her own thoughts.

Or is there something screaming out inside of her, too, to speak?

On Sundays, Tariq and Maajid usually put on clean clothes and ride into Kannapur and go to the mosque for Dhuhr, the prayers of the faithful just after the sun has passed its zenith, just after midday. Although Friday is really our holy day, in India the working week is from Monday to Saturday, and so most Muslims make a point of trying to attend the mosque on Sunday, the only free day of the week. Maajid always says that he would go at dawn, if only he could get up in time. I do not know if they will go today, but I hope that they do, for I will feel better if they go; it might feel, even for a short while, as if everything were normal. Of course, we all know that things are not normal, but then I might talk to Naira – she might feel like talking if the men were out of the house, and I want her to see that I am not her enemy. I want her to see that I am her friend, and that we are family. And I want to know what has happened, so that if there is anything to be done then we can do it, and if there is anything to be said then I might help her to say it. And perhaps we just need to cling to each other for a while, which we have never done before.

Maajid is up before Tariq is. After he has drunk the chai that I give him, he disappears into the storeroom beside the kitchen. A few moments later, he emerges again with some rag, and walks across the courtyard to where his motorbike is leaning over beside the wall, at the end of the latrine nearest to the gate. Soon he is squatting down in the dust beside the bike, and carefully cleaning the dust and the dried mud away from around the wheels and the chain, and then he is polishing the metal here and there. So I know that he, at least, is intending to go to the mosque today. He appears to be in a good mood this morning, and I wonder whether he has decided not to think about the events of yesterday evening. But I wonder what will happen when Tariq appears.

But Tariq does not appear for some time, and when he does it is clear that he is not in a good mood. He comes out of his room a good hour later, dressed only in a lungi; the long cloth tied around his waist and hanging down to his ankles, with the rest of his body uncovered as though he were a labourer, holding a book in one hand. He nods to me as he passes me in the yard, but there is no smile on his face and he says nothing. Naira meets him at the kitchen doorway and hands him his chai, which I think must be cold by now, or has Naira been keeping watch all this time, the chai on the cooker, ready to pour it into the mug when her husband should appear? He takes the chai from her, but they do not speak, and I think that their eyes do not meet. Tariq then walks back across the yard to sit on a chair in the early sunshine near to their room, opens his book, and settles down to read with the chai in one hand. Maajid still polishes his motorbike and appears not to notice any of this.

All of this time, the girls have been mostly in their room. Hana seems to be completely better this morning, and I am feeling an immense relief at this, for at least that is one thing less to worry about. But I know Maajid is worried, despite his appearing to concentrate on cleaning his motorbike and his smiles, since he has not remembered to ask how Hana is, or even gone in to see the girls, as far as I can tell. And this is not like him, because he adores his little daughters. Naira has boiled some eggs and cooked some parathas for breakfast, but so far only the girls seemed to have had any appetite. Hana is making up for the last couple of days, and Leila followed her out and took a paratha, but they both went back to their room after a glance around the courtyard.

There is still a terrible atmosphere in the house.

We need a few things from the shop, and normally I would send Naira out for them. I feel certain, though, that Tariq would object to that, so I decide that I will go myself. The girls are keen to come with me, but I think that if they stay, then there is less likely to be another outbreak of shouting, and so I tell them that I will not be long. I take a basket and as I head for the gateway, Tariq looks up from his book and calls out 'If you are going to the shop will you get me some chips?' And then the girls also want some chips, and Maajid smiles because Tariq has broken his silence, and says 'I'll have some chocolate then, if there is any. I haven't had any chocolate for a while.' So I go out of the gateway and close the gate behind me.

I do not expect Tanu's stall to be open, but there is another small shop about five minutes away. As I pass the old man's stall, I see that the screen is, indeed, across the front, but then I see that it seems as though the chai stall owner has managed to get hold of much of the stock from his neighbour. At the edge of his stall are a couple of sacks, and a few piles of packets and bags, and so I stop there and get some potatoes and some onions and the treats that everyone else had called out for as I was leaving. Then just before I pay, I decide to get an extra bar of chocolate, because I think that if the men do go out, and I am left with Naira and we can talk, then perhaps she would like the chocolate. She has a sweet tooth, and I smile inwardly because I know that she will like it, especially as it is white chocolate which is her favourite. I just hope that she will want to talk to me.

It is late morning before I am certain that both men will go into town to the mosque. Maajid comes out of the storeroom where he has been sorting something, and looks across to where Tariq is still sitting and reading and just says 'Are you nearly ready?' Tariq looks up, and for a moment I think that he is going to say that he is not going to go today, but after a moment he nods and gets up and disappears into his room with his book. He comes out with a towel, goes out to the pump and washes, and comes back and changes into a clean shirt and trousers.

'Okay,' he says, and they get onto the motorbike.

Maajid starts it up, calls out 'Goodbye', and they are gone.

The whole house seems to slowly release its breath. At once the girls bring some toys out of their room and sit down on the veranda to play, while I see Naira very slowly put her head out of the kitchen doorway and look around the yard. I am standing outside the doorway of our room in the shadow of the veranda, and I do not think that she sees me immediately. But then she looks in my direction, and just as quickly looks away again, and I am sure that she has just seen me. Instead of ducking back into the kitchen, however, she remains in the doorway, leaning slightly against the wall and apparently staring into the sky, and I know at once that she is waiting for me to walk across and speak to her. I hesitate for a moment, wondering what it is that I am going to say, and then I go over towards the kitchen.

Naira turns her head towards me as I approach her, but I can read nothing in her face; nothing in her eyes. She waits calmly and impassively as though everything were normal and fine and we were just passing the time of day before settling down to some pleasant activity together. I am just a couple of feet away from her now and I still do not know what I am going to say.

Time slows down.

But Naira is now in control of the situation. 'I have made some more chai, Amma. Sit down, and I will bring it out.' She goes back into the kitchen and, with a feeling of relief, I turn around and go and move one of the chairs so that it is in the sunshine and away from where the girls are playing, and then I fetch a second and place it close beside the first. Almost at once, I move it a few inches away, so that Naira will not feel that I am right on top her, but then I fear that she will think I am keeping my distance, and so I push it back closer again. I am still studying the chairs anxiously when she walks out with the mugs of chai.

'Here you are, Amma. We can sit here for a little while before we need to prepare the lunch.' She sits on the nearest chair and I sit down beside her, feeling unreasonably nervous.

'Thank you,' I say, and then take out the chocolate that I had bought earlier. 'Would you like this with the chai? Everyone else was demanding treats when I went out this morning, so I got this for you.' I hold my breath.

'Oh, thank you!' She smiles. 'My favourite! That *is* kind!' She takes it and unwraps it and then offers me a piece. 'I couldn't eat it all myself.'

'Thank you.' I take the piece and put it in my mouth, but it is dry and powdery, and seems to have no taste. I am not sure whether that is because that is the way that it is, since the chocolate that we get in the village is often old and has been sitting around in the sun for too long, or whether it is because of my nervousness. I chew it with difficulty, feeling all the while that I would like to spit it out but not daring to, fearing that I would be admitting that the chocolate that I had bought as a gift for Naira was old and bad, and that she might think that I had done it deliberately. I was afraid now that she would make a face and spit hers out, but...no. She chews it with a look of pleasure on her face, and sips her chai, and looks across at me and smiles. So now I relax and allow myself to smile, and I try to chew and swallow the chocolate in my own mouth, and I need a large mouthful of chai to do that, larger than I should have taken, and I begin to cough and Naira is all concern, but I manage to control myself and stop and then I have another sip of chai and I am alright.

'Naira...' I begin, when I have stopped coughing, but suddenly I forget what it was I was going to say and I stare at her, holding my cup up just below my chin and wondering how I can finish my sentence but she smiles.

'It is a lovely day after that rain,' she says. 'The air tastes quite fresh, now.' But I see her lip quiver and tears well up in her eyes and this forced normality is all too much for her. She sits still, holding her cup in her hand and staring down at her lap, and soon the tears are running down her face, but she says nothing. Gently, I reach forward and take the cup from her and place it down on the ground. She does not seem to notice. For a while she weeps silently and then she whispers 'It was terrible.'

'What was? What happened?' I ask carefully. She does not look away, and her expression does not change.

'He hit me. And he said that I was a whore.'

'Who did?'

'Tariq.'

'But why would he do that?'

'Because I deserved it.'

'Deserved it? How did you deserve it?' I demand, suddenly angry. She still does not look away, and now her eyes seek mine and hold them and there is that frightening power suddenly present in them again.

'Because I am a whore.' Her voice is cold. 'Because I must have encouraged that man last night.'

'That is ridiculous!' I snap, although even as I do, I realize that I still know nothing of the events the previous afternoon. I pause, then: 'What *did* happen, Naira?' She does not answer at first, and I do not know whether she is trying to remember the details, or summoning the courage to speak, and so I wait. Eventually she begins, and to my surprise she begins by describing the walk to her parents' house, telling me in great detail about the people that she met on the way and that there was quite a lot of traffic on the roads and that she passed one of Tariq's friends who spoke briefly with her. I wait for her to get to the point, not realizing at the time that that is what she is doing.

'My father opened the door when I knocked and, of course, he was surprised to see me. And he was worried that something must be wrong, because why otherwise would I have come? But I said I had just come to visit, and that you were happy that I should come, and so he held the door open for me and called to my mother to make chai. 'Go in to the yard,' he said, 'and take a seat. Have you perhaps come to give us some news?' And I said 'No, not yet, but I hope that it will not be long, and then I will come and tell you, I promise.' 'I pray to Allah that it will be soon', he replied, and then 'What has happened to your face? Come here, Naira, and let me see.'

"It is nothing', I said, as I did not want to make much of it, but he stepped towards me and pulled my scarf away from my face. Then he said 'Who has done this to you? Surely it is not your husband. Perhaps it is your husband's mother?' And I said 'No, no. It was me. I do not know what came over me, and I did it. You must not blame any others.' And then he called my mother and said 'Just come here, for a moment, and look at your daughter's face. How do you suppose that she got these marks?'

'And my mother came into the room, and her smile froze quickly on her face when she saw what was underneath my scarf, and straightaway she said 'I suppose that it was your mother in law who did this to you?' So I said 'No, I have already explained to Father that I did it. I was feeling that I had the blame for everything that went wrong, and that I could do nothing right.' And it is true, Amma, that I did feel that way, and I think now that it is natural, and that I should have had more patience, but I said 'No, Mama, it was me. I did it to myself.'

'My parents did not want to believe me, but I suppose also that they did not want to believe it might be someone else in our family, and I could see that they were unhappy. They left me sitting in the yard, and went and had words in the kitchen that I was not to hear, and then they brought out the chai. They sat down and my father said 'We will say no more about it, for it is not our concern any longer.' Then we talked of other things; of my brothers, and what my parents had done, and that my father's brother had died, which I had not heard, which saddened me. But then it was time to leave, and I said 'It will be getting dark, soon, and I must go,' then suddenly my parents seemed to be worried again, and were reluctant to let me go, and I almost had to insist. And this meant that when I did leave, it was later than I had intended to leave, and I had to hurry along the lane.'

She fell silent again, and dropped her head so that she looked at her hands resting in her lap, and it was a while before she spoke again.

'I had not gone very far,' she continued, 'when a man stepped out of a side street. I thought nothing of this until he called me, and I looked across at him and I saw that it was that same friend of Tariq's who I had met on the way to my parents. 'Wait,' he said, 'there was something I was going to ask you.' He stepped a little closer. 'Who has done that thing to your face? Was it your husband?' I tried to ignore him and walk on, but he followed me closely and said 'Wait!' again. When I looked around, I could not see anyone else and I began to feel a little afraid, although I knew that this man was a friend of my husband, so I told myself that there was no need to be. Then he was in front of me, and I could smell his breath, and I think that he might have been drinking. Now he said again 'Was it Tariq?' 'No,' I said. 'Of course not!' 'If you were my wife, I would not do that to you!' he said, and now I was definitely frightened. 'You seem in a hurry,' he said. 'Slow down. Why don't you come and take a drink with me?' And he took a bottle out from his pocket and showed it to me, although I don't know what it was.

"No', I said, 'I am on my way home. Excuse me.' and I tried to walk past him, but he kept moving this way and that, so that he was constantly in front of me and in my way and I could not get past, and I said 'Please, let me go.' 'I am not stopping you,' he said. 'I cannot get past,' I replied. 'You are not fast enough,' he laughed, and then he took me by the wrist and said 'What is the hurry? Just have a little drink,' and he held up the bottle again, but I pulled my arm from him and I managed to get away from his hold and I ran off suddenly to the side before he could grab me again and I thought that I had managed to get past him, but he was faster than me and then he was in front of me again and when I tried to run off to the side again I found myself in an alleyway between some houses and the tea stall and I could not see the way out up ahead of me, and so I slowed down slightly and then he caught up with me.'

I can hear her voice rising, and I think that she is going to cry again, although I am also afraid that she might become hysterical, but then she stops, and her eyes are staring into mine, and I have no idea what to say, and so I just say 'And then what happened?' I immediately think that she might lose control, and that I have said the wrong thing, but she swallows and continues.

'He tried to grab my wrist, but I pulled my hand away, although it hurt my arm and I ran again, but just as I reached the front of the tea stall he caught me, and then he held me by the wrist again and pushed me against the wall of the tea stall and when I opened my mouth to shout out or scream he was pushing against me and he kissed me hard, so painfully hard, Amma, I thought that he was biting me and I could feel his thing pushing against me.' She begins to cry, now. 'I could feel him hard against me and I did scream then, even though his mouth was over mine and that forced him to move his face and he was suddenly very angry and he began to speak again but I didn't hear what he said because I was screaming and I felt his hand grab at me...' she jumps up suddenly from the chair, and runs across the yard into the latrine, and I can hear her retching and spitting, but I cannot move from my seat. I glance across the veranda to see that the girls have gone back into their room again, and I think 'Thank God they have done that. I should have sent them back in before we started talking. I wonder how much they heard.'

Eventually Naira comes back out again and walks slowly across the yard towards me, stands for a moment silently looking into the distance, it seems, and then slowly sits down again. I look at her and open my mouth to speak but she anticipates what I was going to say.

'I'm alright. I must tell you all this, Amma. He...he dragged me towards Tanu's stall, and pushed me against the screen and I fell back and it collapsed and he fell on top of me, and now I could feel his hands...' she stares at me for a while without speaking, but her eyes, which are ever so wide open and unblinking are not looking at me, at least I don't think that she sees me, and then she continues 'but then I think that someone must have heard me scream and a man's voice shouted out, 'What's going on?' and this other man, the one who had pulled me into the stall, put his hand over my mouth but didn't say anything and I could feel his breath on my face and I was terrified and I didn't know what I was doing so I bit his hand and then he yelled out and moved his hand and I screamed again and this time there were voices outside and he jumped quickly up off of me and ran off and then there were people standing near me but I got to my feet and this time I ran as fast as I could and I don't think he followed me this time, because I'm sure that he could have caught me if he had and he didn't so maybe the other people scared him and then I was back here.' She stops. We sit together, neither speaking, Naira's head lowered again, seemingly looking at her hands which are constantly moving; fingers twining around each other and her nails picking at each other and occasionally scratching her palm or the back of her hand – I find myself watching them, too. Then I look up at her.

'So, he didn't…he didn't…' She looks up and her eyes meet mine, but now she appears to be calm.

'No, he didn't, although it was all horrible enough. He didn't. But Tariq does not believe me. And if he came after me it must be my fault because somehow I tempted him.'

I look at her for a moment or two without speaking and then, almost without realizing what I am doing, I reach out and take her hand. She does not resist me, and we sit this way for a while. 'Of course it is not your fault, Naira. I do not believe it when men say these things. I think that they say them to excuse their own bad behaviour.' She does not reply at once, but looks at me thoughtfully.

'Amma,' she says at last, 'I wanted to tell you something yesterday or the day before, but you were busy, and then I changed my mind but I think I must tell you now. I should have told Tariq first, I suppose, which is why I changed my mind but I did not get a chance to tell him and that is why I did not tell my parents either…' she stops and looks at me uncertainly.

'Go on.' I say.

'Well, Amma, I…I think that I may be pregnant!'

'But this is wonderful news!' I exclaim, getting to my feet. She looks up at me, still holding my hand, but does not say anything more.

'Is it?' she finally says.

'But of course!' I am astonished by her reaction. 'How could it not be?' She slowly, gently, withdraws her hand from mine and places it in her lap on top of the other hand.

'I fear that Tariq will not think so.'

'Tariq? Why would he not think so? It is what he wants! It is what we all want! Naira, it is wonderful news! All of this will be forgotten when you tell him this news!'

'Will it?' she says, and gives a little laugh in which there is not the least trace of humour. 'Will it? I fear very much that he will say that it is not his.'

'Naira! No!'

'I should have told him before. I should have made time. I should have made him listen. It wouldn't have taken long, I could have told him before he went to work. Oh, why didn't I tell him? Now he will not believe me.'

'Of course he will, Naira!'

'Oh, Amma, he will not. I know that he will not.' I look at her, and then I have another thought.

'Naira, does he know yet that the man yesterday was his friend?'

'No, I did not tell him that.' We look at each other and I see tears in her eyes, again. Then, she looks around the yard and turns back to me. 'They will be back from town, soon, Amma. We must prepare lunch.' I nod, slowly. She is right. We must prepare lunch.

NINE

I do not know what it was that the Imam was preaching at the mosque, or whether Maajid had been talking to him while they were out, but when Maajid and Tariq return, Tariq appears to be relaxed and happy. He is smiling at us all, and even speaking civilly to Naira. The lunch is not quite ready, so I apologize and say that we have been busy, and Maajid smiles and says nothing, but Tariq waves his hand and says 'No problem, no problem. I will go and see my sisters. I want to see that Hana is better now.'

He drinks some water, and goes to sit with them for a while as they play on the veranda. I can see that they are happy to have his attention, and Maajid just says to me 'That is good. I will go and change. I feel a bit dry and dusty after sitting in the mosque and riding back. I will put on something looser. Can you get me a drink of water?'

He goes off to our room, and I go and get a glass of water and take it to him. He looks up as I come in, and says 'He is still very angry, but he has agreed to be respectful, because I have told him that I will not have our house turned into a battlefield and that he must listen to what Naira has to say and,' he sighs, 'I just hope that I have said the right thing.'

'I am sure that you have,' I reply. 'And I am glad that you have said it. I was worried about Naira because I did not think that he had treated her fairly.'

'She is his wife,' Maajid replies, his voice suddenly frosty, 'and it is up to him how he treats her. However, he has a duty to hear her out. If she has behaved improperly, then it is his right to chastise her as he sees fit. We will see. And now, we will say nothing more on the subject.'

And then, I am suddenly desperate to do something, to say something, to help Naira, and I almost tell Maajid that she has told me that she believes herself to be pregnant. And it is all that I can do to stop myself from blurting it out, but first she must tell Tariq herself. It is not our business until then. And so I give Maajid his cup of water, and I turn and go and return to the kitchen where the meal is almost ready. I help Naira to finish what needs doing then go to the doorway and call Tariq and the girls and say, 'Tariq, just go and call your father, too.' And by the time that we bring out the food, everyone is on the veranda and sitting down, and they are talking while they wait for us. Tariq is explaining something to Leila for her schoolwork, and Maajid is saying something quietly to Hana, but they all stop when the food appears.

I cannot help but notice that Tariq looks at Naira as she puts down the food on the veranda, but that she seems not to want to look at him at the moment. I think Oh Naira, he will think that you are feeling guilty if you do that! But of course she *is* feeling guilty, and so that is exactly what she does. I feel that I want to scream, but I put down the plates and go to fetch some water and some metal cups. When I come back, Naira is seated next to Tariq and I think at least she is sitting next to him, but then I think perhaps it is so that she does not have to catch his eye. But then I am cross with myself and think oh, don't think the worst! But there are no arguments or unpleasantness during the meal, and although the atmosphere feels tense and awkward, we get through it safely.

After lunch is over and Naira and I have cleared away, I go out into the yard and see Maajid seated on one of the chairs in the sun with his eyes closed. I do not know whether he is dozing or not, but when I get near him he opens his eyes and looks at me, and says, 'Tariq has gone out. He has not said where.'

I am about to ask him whether he thinks he knows who it was that assaulted Naira, but I fear that she may come out of the kitchen behind me and overhear this, so I say nothing except 'Is there anything that you want?' and he replies 'No.' and closes his eyes again, so I go off to see what the girls are doing.

They are both in their room playing with their dolls, brushing their hair and changing their dresses. I ask Hana whether she feels alright still, and she replies 'Yes, Mama.'

And then I ask Leila if she has had any pains or sickness, and she replies 'No, nothing.'

So I am relieved, but I still have a suspicion at the back of my mind, but I think that I will let that be for the moment. So I just say to Leila 'Do you have any homework to do for tomorrow?'

She makes a face and says 'just a little bit, Mama, I will do it later.'

'No, come on, do it now, or it will get forgotten and then you will have to do it in the morning before breakfast and it will not happen.'

We go out on the veranda, and I sit with my back against the storeroom wall while Leila does her work. I feel tired, and my eyelids droop, and I must have fallen asleep, because Naira is standing at the gate with a man who I have never seen before and she says 'This is my new husband, Amma.' I say 'But what of Tariq?' and she looks puzzled and says 'That was not my fault. He does not seem to want me anymore. I will have a baby with this one.'

I sit up, shocked, and Naira is standing in front of me with a cup of water. 'Here, Amma. It has become hot, now.' She hands me the cup, which I take and I nod to her without speaking, because I feel a little confused. When I look up, I see Maajid drinking also from a cup, and Leila has disappeared, leaving her exercise book and pencil on the ground beside me. I pick up the book and look at what she has done, and see that she has been working hard while I was asleep, and so I get to my feet and go and give it to her and say 'Well done, Leila. That looks alright.' And because I am still feeling sleepy, I go into our room and lie down on my bedroll and quickly fall asleep.

I am woken later by Naira, who is standing at the door looking in at me. There is a slight breeze now, which is refreshingly cool. Naira says 'It is time to begin the supper, Amma. I will start now. There is no need to hurry.' And she is gone.

When I leave the room, the first person I see is Maajid. He is still sitting in the courtyard, but he has moved his chair round so that he is still in the sun, and now he is reading a book. 'Is Tariq back, yet?' I ask him.

He looks up and hesitates for a moment, before replying 'No, not yet,' and then goes back to his book. I am not sure how long it is that I have been asleep, but the sun is now much lower in the sky and I wonder if I am wrong to feel a bit worried that Tariq has not returned. If Maajid is worried, though, he is hiding it well, so perhaps there is no need.

It is dusk before Tariq returns, just as the supper is ready. I am relieved he is back, and back in time to eat, although I am still worried that he had been away for so long. He does not seem to be in a very good mood now, though, and he speaks little to us and is sharp with his answers. When the food is out, he sits down on the veranda beside the lamp and helps himself to the various dishes without speaking, and then eats quickly without looking up at the rest of us. As soon as he has finished, he gets up wordlessly and goes out to the pump to wash his hands, and then goes into his room. His mood has affected the girls who are unusually silent, and Maajid glances at me every now and again, although I do not know what these glances can mean.

When the meal is over, and we begin to get to our feet Maajid says 'Hana, Leila, you can help Naira clear away.' 'Yes, Baba.' I know that he intends to speak to me, and Naira glances at me for it must be clear to her, too, but they clear away, and Maajid and I walk across the yard and stand in the shadow by the gate.

Maajid's voice is low. 'I think that Tariq has been drinking. I am sure that I could smell it on his breath. I hope that does not mean that he will behave badly, because I can see that he is already in an ill humour. I do not know where he has been this afternoon, but I hope also that he has not been spreading around any news that we should be keeping to ourselves. Sometimes, when men drink, they do not exercise proper control over their tongues.'

'What can we do?'

'Nothing,' he replies. 'He will do what he will do, but I pray that he does not do anything foolish.'

There is really nothing else to say, and we stand there in silence. I am surprised, then, when Maajid suddenly puts a hand to my face and gently strokes my hair beneath my scarf. 'Allah will watch over us,' he says. 'I am going to go to bed, because I am tired.' And he steps away and I watch him go.

Tariq appears at the doorway of his room as Maajid returns from the pump, and Maajid sees him and changes direction to go to speak to his son, but Tariq ducks back into his room, leaving Maajid standing at the edge of the veranda uncertainly. I am still standing nearby and he glances at me, and then steps forward and goes into Tariq's room. Feeling somehow that I should not stay where I am, in case anyone should think that I am trying to overhear what is being said, I go into the kitchen to see if everyone has finished tidying away. We will not clean the dishes until the morning, for it is dark in the courtyard where we clean them with ashes and water, and we prefer not to go out to the pump after dark, if it can be helped. They are just finishing, and I give the girls a pot of water and tell them to go and brush their teeth and get to bed. When they have gone out, I look at Naira and ask her how she feels. For a moment she does not answer, but then she steps forward, puts her arms around me and I feel the pressure of her body and her cheek against mine. Then she steps away and goes outside. Slightly startled, I stand still for a moment, and then follow her out.

As I fetch my toothbrush, Naira goes into her room and I wait for a moment to see if she should come out again immediately, and when she does not I assume that Maajid must have already had a word with Tariq and gone to bed, unless Tariq would not speak to him in the first place, of course. Quickly brushing my teeth, I go to the girls' room to make certain that they are settling down, and then go to our room. Maajid is sitting on his bedroll in bare feet, unbuttoning his shirt. 'What did he say?' I ask. Maajid shrugs.

'He says that he was making enquiries this afternoon. When I asked what that meant, he would not say anything more.' I sit down beside him.

'What do you think he meant by that?'

'I don't know. I don't know who he has been talking to.' He puts his hands down behind him and leans back slightly, staring up at the ceiling. 'Everybody knows everything about everyone in a village. Even if he chooses not to tell us anything, we will hear all about it soon enough.' He looks around at me. 'And I daresay that you will hear enough tomorrow when you go out. Women are always the first to spread gossip.' I say nothing. 'Talking of which,' he continues, I would imagine that you and Naira had plenty to talk about while we were at the mosque, today. I am sure that she has told you more than she said last night when she came home.'

'Perhaps a little more,' I say, guardedly. 'She was late coming home because her parents were worried about her face and didn't want her to go.' I immediately regret saying this, but he merely continues to look at me, and so I continue. 'And when she did leave it was getting dark and a man tried to stop her and offered her liquor, and then he grabbed her wrist and it seems he was trying to drag her off somewhere, but she managed to get free and run off.'

'Did she say who it was?'

'No,' I lie, immediately.

'And that was it? That doesn't sound so terrible.'

'It might not to you,' I say angrily, 'but you are not a woman!' He waves a hand lightly in the air.

'No, no, that's not what I mean. I meant it is not so much for Tariq to be angry about, if indeed that is all that happened. Was that all?'

'I think so.'

Before he can answer, voices are suddenly raised in the next room; there is an angry shout that is clearly from Tariq, a scream, and then a crash. Immediately after this there are footsteps on the veranda and, while I seem to be frozen with fear and feel a dreadful sickness, Maajid is on his feet and out of the room, and I hear his voice which is cut off by Tariq shouting angrily again, and the sound of the gate opening and then crashing closed again, and then a silence, in which I can just hear Naira crying.

I finally get to my feet, and stumble out of the doorway. I look quickly around the yard, which appears to be empty, and then look in the doorway. Naira is lying on the floor on her side, and in the light of the lamp on the trunk by the window, I see that she seems to be bleeding from the corner of her mouth. I am relieved to see that she is conscious and weeping, and I stoop down but have no idea what to say, but she looks up at me without speaking and I finally say 'I will get a cloth for your face, Naira,' and get to my feet and go out of the room.

As I cross the yard towards the kitchen, I hear weeping from the girls' room and so I quickly change direction and look in. The room is in darkness, so I call softly 'Are you awake?'

Hana replies 'Yes, Mama.'

'What has happened?' asks Leila.

'Naira has fallen over, but she is alright. Now go to sleep.' I then hurry to the kitchen, light the lamp and find a clean cloth, soak it in water, and return to Naira. She is now sitting up, and has wiped her mouth with her hand, so that the blood is smeared across her face and on her hand. She is staring at the blood on her hand, and some more is dripping from her chin onto her clothes. I lean forward quickly and wipe her chin to try to stop the drips, and I still do not know what to say, but she has stopped weeping and looks to be shocked.

'You will ruin all of your clothes if you cover them in blood,' I say, and then think why on earth did I say something stupid like that? But she laughs unexpectedly.

'I must stop doing it. I seem to be making rather a habit of it! Thank you, Amma. Please give me the cloth.' She takes it and wipes her mouth, and then looks at it and says 'I told him everything.'

'Even about being pregnant?' I ask.

'No, not that. I did not have a chance. But he knows that it was his friend, and he said he did not believe me, and that I was a liar, and he hit me. But then he said 'I will find out the truth' and now he has gone.'

I hear the gate open and close, and I get to my feet and go to look out of the doorway. Just before I reach it, I glance back to see Naira staring wide-eyed at me. Looking out, I see Maajid approaching the doorway, and that he appears to be alone.

'I couldn't catch him,' he says, and I hear that he is breathing heavily. 'I lost sight of him at the end of the street and I don't know where he went. I looked around for a while, but couldn't see him and then I began to think that I looked rather suspicious and thought that I'd better come back.' He makes no attempt to look past me. 'Is Naira alright?'

'I think so. I don't really know what has happened, yet.'

'Well, I will go and put some water on,' he says, unexpectedly. 'I could do with a drink, and I suppose that both of you would like one, too. You talk to Naira. She might know where he has gone.' He crosses the yard, and as he goes I listen out for any sounds from the girls' room, but can hear nothing. So after standing still for a few more moments, I turn around and go back into Naira's room where I see that she has laid down again, and although I am standing in front of her, it seems as though she does not see me, for she says nothing and her eyes seem to be staring into the far distance somewhere that I cannot see.

'Naira,' I say softly, but her eyes do not move and she does not reply. 'Naira!' a little louder, now, but still there is no reaction, and I have no idea whether or not she hears me, or has simply decided not to acknowledge my presence.

Suddenly I worry that she might be unconscious, so I step forward and crouch down in front of her, meaning to shake her gently, but as I do so she looks into my face and dully says 'Please leave me alone, now. There is nothing that you can do.' She then turns over to face away from me and so, after a little hesitation, I get back to my feet and turn and walk out and go to the kitchen to join Maajid.

'What did she say?' he asks.

'Nothing. She does not want to talk, and I do not suppose that I could make her do so. Let us sit on the veranda and wait for Tariq to come back. I am worried what he might do.' Maajid nods.

'I am, too,' he says, simply, and in the light of the lantern he suddenly looks much older than usual. We say nothing more as we wait for the chai to boil, and once it has done then Maajid tips it into the cups and we go outside and sit down and we still do not speak.

After a while I get up and go and fetch blankets. I hand one to Maajid who nods at me, and takes it and wraps it around his shoulders, but still does not speak, and I sit down and do likewise. I hear all of the night noises, now, the barking of the dogs, the crickets; in the distance there is a vehicle of some sort droning as it labours its way from somewhere to somewhere else, and I find myself straining my ears to hear the different sounds that it makes. I picture it slowing down for bends, or to negotiate a particularly rough part of the road, and I wonder if it is coming towards the village. But for a while it seems to get neither louder nor quieter, and I decide that this must be because it is going along a road that passes the village, without coming near. As I work that out, the sounds do begin to get quieter, and then eventually disappear altogether.

Maybe because I have been listening so hard, all the other sounds seem to be much louder than they were before. Then there is a voice nearby, and I raise my head quickly, and Maajid does also, but there are no footsteps or other sounds, then there are no other voices, and we relax again; or maybe not relax, no, that is the wrong word. We sit back again, and perhaps our muscles soften and we sag, yes, we sag again as we sit leaning against the wall, but we are both alert, listening for any sounds that might signify the return of our son.

The night wears on, and after what seems to be many hours, I ask Maajid the time and he replies that it has just gone eleven o'clock. I think that it must be later than that, but I am sure that his watch is right, and now I am very worried and I cannot stop wondering where Tariq is and what he has been doing. Even if he has confronted this fellow who is supposed to be his friend, and they have had an argument and perhaps a fight, then he surely should have been back by now. But what if they have killed each other? Now I am being foolish, I tell myself. But perhaps he is walking around the village somewhere, trying to clear his head or thinking what should he do? I wonder whether to suggest to Maajid that he should go out again to look for him, but no sooner do I think this, than I think that it is better that we wait for his return. He cannot be out all night for he has to go to work in the morning.

The night wears on. Maajid now softly tells me to take my blanket and go and lie down and sleep. 'I will sit up some more,' he says. 'If he has not come back in another hour or so, I will...well, I'm not sure what I will do. Perhaps I will come in also and try to go to sleep and go out in the morning to look for him if he is still not back.' So I hesitate and then I say 'Alright. Wake me up if he returns.' And I get up and go and lie down on my bedroll, not expecting to go to sleep, but the next thing that I know is that daylight is creeping through the window.

TEN

I lie still, conscious that something important, something monumental, has happened, but unable to recall for the moment what it might be. All seems to be as it should be; Maajid snores beside me, and along with the pale daylight creeping in through the window, there come the reassuring morning sounds of birdsong. I turn over and check the time, and find that we have slept late. I throw off the blanket and begin to get to my feet. It is at that point that I remember what has happened, and I drop back down to my knees, overbalancing slightly and putting one hand down to steady myself while with the other I shake the shoulder of my sleeping husband. 'Maajid!' I hiss, urgently. 'Maajid! Did he come back last night?'

Maajid opens his eyes and looks at me blearily 'No. I didn't see him.' He closes his eyes again, and then before I can say anything else opens them again and groans gently. 'Allah, I'm tired. I sat up until four. Give me another hour and then come and wake me.'

He shuts his eyes and seems to be immediately asleep again. I cannot move; I kneel beside him and gently stroke his hair for a moment, until I realize that I am weeping. Then I think to myself I have to get the children up to go to school. I must go and get the fire lit and I wonder how Naira is today. And what if Tariq is outside? I think suddenly. What if he came back during the night and did not want to wake everyone up? It is a ridiculous thought but I leap to my feet and run bare-footed to the gate and pull it open and step outside and look up and down the street and he is not there so I go round the corner and then a little way further and I stare into the distance and wring my hands and then turn and run back the other way around the corner again and along the alleyway to the next road but there is nothing.

There is no sign of him.

I return slowly and heavily and then stand at the gate for what seems to be a long time, looking up and down the road, until I remember the fire and go back inside and close the gate, then go into the kitchen and set the kindling and take out a match and light the fire. And then I am aware that Naira is standing behind me, so I fix a smile on my face and turn around slowly, but anything that I had thought to say dies on my lips as I see her terrible face and its expression.

I am unable to speak, but she says in a flat, lifeless voice 'He is not back, then.'

'No,' I say, eventually. There is a silence that I feel I have to break. 'But I'm sure he will be soon!' I blurt out and she smiles coldly and shakes her head.

'No, he won't. Something has happened, don't you see?' I stare at her, and icy tingles run down my back.

'What do you mean? What has happened?'

'I don't know,' she replies, 'but if he is not back, then it is my fault, because none of this would have happened but for me.'

'Naira, no!' I gasp. 'You know that is not true!' She opens her eyes wide and stares at me without blinking.

'It *is* true! It *is* my fault!'

I am frightened. The other Naira seems to have returned.

'It is not your fault!' I manage to say, more firmly than I had expected. 'Naira, go and wash your face and take a chair and sit down and I will bring you some chai. It won't take long. Please, Naira!' She stares at me for a moment with those wild staring eyes, but then she turns and walks softly out and I hear the click of the gate. Only then do I reach for a cloth, and as I wipe my eyes I think of the fresh blood that was running down her face where she must have opened her wounds again with her nails. I want Maajid to wake up and be with me, because I am scared for Naira and for Tariq, and I am scared for me and for all of us, but he needs to sleep and so I do not go to wake him. Instead, I put all the ingredients for the chai in the pan except for the water, and then I quickly go to look in at the girls. They are still asleep, and so I think I will leave them a little longer, and at least Naira is washing her face and so they won't see what I have just seen.

The fire is drawing through, and I take a pot and then hesitate, because I don't want to go out and fetch water while Naira is at the pump, partly because I am afraid to see her at the moment, but partly also because she would expect to be asked to fetch the water. Although it is saving her a task, I am fearful that she will resent me for it; as though by doing so I would be indicating that I did not think her capable at the moment, and so I wait, wondering at the same time why she is taking so long. Eventually I hear the click of the gate again, and so I go out of the doorway with the pot and say 'Oh, Naira, since you're there would you just fetch the water for the chai?'

She smiles slightly and says 'Of course,' and takes the pot and goes out again. She is soon back, and she hands me the pot and then disappears into her room. I go into the kitchen and pour the water into the pan with the chai and put it over the fire, and when I look out again, she is sitting in one of the chairs just outside her doorway.

Outside, I suddenly hear footsteps hurrying along the road and I look up quickly, my heart in my mouth, wondering whether it might be Tariq. But Naira does not shift her gaze from her lap, and maybe she does not hear the footsteps, or perhaps she just knows they are not Tariq's. Then I realize that no, while they are obviously not his, perhaps they might belong to someone who has come with news of him, good or ill, and I cannot bear not to know! They pass, however, and fade away into all the other sounds that are outside the house. I force myself to stay in the kitchen, getting out pans and moving them about the kitchen so that I think we will be ready for breakfast, although after a while I have moved the same pans around so many times that I have completely forgotten which ones we will need or what I had intended that we would eat. But then the chai has boiled, and I quickly stir it to make sure that the sugar has all dissolved, and take a mug out to Naira, who is still seated in the chair outside her room. She looks up as I approach, and I am relieved when she says 'Oh, thank you. That looks good.' And takes it with both hands and sips it, and then sits holding it in her lap smiling gently.

I tiptoe back to the kitchen and wonder whether an hour has gone past yet, but decide that even if it hasn't, then Maajid would probably welcome chai. I pour his and, as I am about to take it out to him, there is a disturbance outside the gate. Thinking it might be Tariq, I leave the cup and run across the yard and pull the gate open. As I do, a woman outside falls to her knees and throws her arms around my legs, almost knocking me to the ground. At first, I cannot make out what she is saying, since all of her words are virtually lost in her distraught wailing, but now a man runs up and stops just behind her, puffing furiously, and as he is trying to catch his breath he lifts his hand and points a trembling finger at me. He is trying hard to say something, but is not yet able to.

The woman is now weeping, and has buried her head in my sari, but the man has got his breath back. 'My son has been taken away by the police! Your son, he came around and made a fuss and caused a fight and then the police came and arrested them and he did nothing wrong, it was your son he was disturbing the neighbours and there were children crying in the next house and someone must have gone to tell the police, because soon they were there and they arrested them both and took them off to Kannapur.' He stops, and I can hear the woman still weeping. I have stepped backwards while the man is speaking, and now his wife is left crouching on the ground, her arms resting on the ground before her and her head on her arms. I can just see a little of the side of her face, enough to see that her eyes are closed, and I am struggling to take in what has been said. Although there are many noises outside in the village, we seem for the moment to be trapped inside a bubble of silence. All that I can see is the side of the woman's face.

Then Naira appears at my shoulder; I feel her presence, and the man is now looking at her, and there is hatred in his eyes and he is suddenly reanimated with a furious anger. 'She is the cause of all of this! This woman accused my son of molesting her! Why should he do that? Why would he do that? She is a filthy Moslem; he would be defiled! He is engaged to be married to a nice Hindu girl! I shall go to the village council!' He takes a step or two forward and raises his hand as if to slap her but then stops, and he seems to get control of himself. He looks at me again and I think I see fear in his eyes 'Oh, please, you must go to the police! Tell them that it is all a mistake! We are neighbours; we live in the same village as you! They have taken your son, too! What are we to do?'

Helplessly, I turn towards where Naira was standing, but she has disappeared into the house and I see Maajid shuffling across the courtyard, watched by Leila and Hana. Whether the girls have woken him, or he has heard the commotion, I have no idea, but we all now stand in silence watching him approach the gate. Even the woman on her knees has stopped her wailing and is sitting back and watching and time seems to pass very, very slowly. And then finally Maajid reaches the gate, and he puts out an arm and leans wearily against the post and looks from one person to another, and then asks very softly 'What is this?'

I open my mouth to speak, but at the same time the man at the gate, our neighbour, opens his too and says 'I...' and then stops and looks at me and then back at Maajid who looks back at him and asks in the same soft voice 'Do you know where my son is, then?'

There is another long silence, but then the man seems to draw himself up a little taller and says 'Yes, yes I do. The police have arrested him. He came to my house and he caused a disturbance. He threatened my son...'

'Threatened?' says Maajid, mildly, but the man immediately looks uncertain. Suddenly I want to know exactly what was said between Tariq and this other young man. Although Maajid is tired, he also notices how this man's manner has suddenly changed, and he says 'So you heard what they said, did you?'

'Well,' the man replies, 'not all of it, I...'

'So what did you hear?'

'Your son threatened Satyak, he threatened my son...'

'Threatened? What did he say?' The man seems almost to cringe, now,

'He threatened to go to the police,' he says eventually.

'Why?' asks Maajid, 'why would he do that?'

'He...it was a mistake, I am sure...' Now he can no longer look Maajid in the face, but glances at me and then down at his wife and swallows before continuing '...He said that he thought that my son had molested his wife, but that is nonsense and if it happened at all it must have been another man. Why would my son want to do that? It is ridiculous!'

'Perhaps we had better both go and see the police' says Maajid.

'What?' exclaims the other man. 'Why would I want to go with you?'

'Maybe they will take more notice if there are two of us. This should not be our quarrel for we both want to find out what has happened to our sons. And if there are things to be said then we can say them when we both know the truth.'

This other man is obviously still uncertain, and I think perhaps he does not trust Maajid. But he is afraid for his son, just as we are afraid for Tariq, and I am suddenly sorry for him and for his wife, who still squats silently and uncertainly on her heels at the gate, taking no part in this conversation. I think that I can see tears in her eyes, and before I realize what I am doing I step forward and I touch her sleeve and I say 'Come inside and sit and have chai while our husbands go to see what has become of our sons.'

She looks up at me as if she does not understand, and looks then at her husband who says 'That is okay. You stay here and we will be back soon.' And it is decided. Maajid starts the motorbike and, after a glance at me, he goes off with the other man sitting behind him.

When the woman is seated on a chair, I go to the kitchen where I find Naira sitting on the floor and leaning back against the wall, looking sullen and angry. 'Why did you ask that woman into our house?' I do not know what to answer. 'I do not want her here,' she continues.

'But why?' I eventually get out. 'She has done us no harm.'

'It was her son who molested me,' she replies.

'I know,' I say in return, 'but she is frightened, too, as I am. As we all are. I do not know what is going to happen, and I do not want to make an enemy of her.'

'Well I don't want to see her or talk to her.'

'Then stay here, if you must.' I reply, suddenly exasperated. 'I will take the chai to her.' And I take the mug that I was going to have and I pour some out, but Naira stands up while I am doing this, and takes another mug down from the shelf and hands it to me. And then while I am pouring out this second mug, she takes the first one and goes outside. Through the doorway I see her hand it to the other woman and then continue across the yard and go into her room without speaking.

And then I hear Daanish arrive at the gate and I think Oh, the girls! I had not given a thought to them while all of this was going on. I rush out of the kitchen, but they are both coming out of their room and I say 'Have you got any money?'

Leila says 'I have, Mama, it is alright.'

So I hurry over to kiss them, and then I say 'Oh, you have not had any breakfast!'

'Don't worry, Mama. We will be alright.' I look back towards the kitchen, wondering if there is anything I could give them to eat on the way, but Hana opens the gate, and we all go outside and they get into the auto which then drives off. I stand watching it until it disappears round the corner, and then turn round and go back into the courtyard, closing the gate behind me, to see that the woman is watching me unhappily. I pause, and then go back to the kitchen to fetch my drink, then go out and cross over to where she is sitting and stand beside her. I look at her, but she has now turned away from me and is looking anywhere except at me or towards where Naira has disappeared, and after a moment I say 'What is your name?'

She looks up at me and she doesn't speak at first, but her eyes bore into mine and I feel uncomfortable, but then quickly she looks away and says, clearly enough, 'I am Kaushalya, which means mother of Rama.' She looks back at me again. 'Do you know who Rama was?' I nod my head, but she continues 'he was a hero; a man who was incapable of doing wrong!' She intimidates me with her gaze, and I do not know how to answer what she says.

'I am Siddiqa.' I say eventually. 'It means honest.' She looks at me coolly, and then lifts her mug to her lips and sips at the chai, but then she looks away again, her defiance dissolving. I do not know what to do, but eventually I fetch another of the chairs and I place it carefully alongside hers – not too close, but not so far away that it would appear unfriendly, and I think Hai Allah! It is just like it was yesterday with Naira, but Naira does not want to be a part of this today. I fear that it may be a long time before our husbands return, and I do not know what we can talk about, so I sit down and try to smile at her, although she is deliberately not looking in my direction, and take a sip of my own chai.

I want to ask her how many children she has, because this is what we women all ask each other, but that will draw attention to her son. And so I hold my tongue and bite my lip, and put my hand to my mouth, and now I have a slight but rising feeling almost of panic, because I fear we shall be sitting here for hours and the tension will prove too much for one or both of us, and we might scream or shout or come to blows. But then she turns to face me and puts her mug down on the ground. 'I will go back home and wait for my husband. Thank you for the chai.' She gets to her feet and goes and opens the gate, and walks out without a backward glance.

I slowly let out a long, long breath and then turn around to look towards Naira's room. I realize that I am expecting to see her come out into the yard now, but she does not appear. I wonder if that is because she does not realize that the woman has left, or simply because she is sulking, or still angry with me, or even perhaps because she has fallen asleep. So in the end I get up and I pick up the other mug, and I go into the kitchen.

When Maajid returns, I am sitting on the veranda outside our room, mending the seam in a pair of his trousers. At the sound of the motorbike I look up, and the engine slows and quietens, and then I see the gate open and Maajid looks in at me.

'She has gone home' I say, and he nods and goes back outside, and after a moment or two I watch him drive in through the gateway. He parks the bike, and very slowly and deliberately balances the machine on the stand, and then swings his leg over the top and stands looking down at the ground by his feet for a few moments. I glance across the yard to see Naira standing in her doorway watching him. No one speaks. Eventually he looks across at me and I know that he has no good news to bring, and the question I was about to ask hangs unspoken in the air before me like a ghost. Softly Naira appears at my side like another sad ghost. She sits down on the veranda next to me as Maajid walks across the yard and squats down in the dust facing us.

'It is just as we thought,' he says at last. 'They are at the police station, but we were not allowed to see them, and we could not find out anything else. They wouldn't tell us anything, and even denied that either of the boys were there at first and told us to go away. When we insisted, they finally agreed that they were there, but said that we couldn't see them, because they had been arrested. We weren't even allowed to know what they've been charged with.' He looks at us both and shrugs slightly. 'I don't know what we do now, but this other fellow says he is going back later with some other family members so perhaps I should go, too.' *'I will go as well, then,'* says Naira quickly, but Maajid says firmly 'No, that would not be a good idea.' And Naira hangs her head and looks a little bit sulky again, but Maajid just says 'I am going to go and lie down for an hour; I am still very tired. I know where that family live, now, so I'll go over after I have eaten and find out when they are planning to go back to the police station.'

ELEVEN

That afternoon Maajid goes back to the police station at the same time as the other family go, and then the next morning he goes twice again. The second time he goes, I go with him, but the police refuse to tell us anything. Maajid says on the way back that was just like yesterday, and we spend the rest of the day pretending that everything is normal because there is not much else that we can do, other than talk about it over and over again and I do not want to do that, especially in front of the girls who are as upset as we are.

We are about to bring out the dishes for supper, when I hear the sound of a vehicle pulling up behind the house. Almost immediately there is a loud knocking at the gate. I want to put down what I am holding, and rush out to see if it is Tariq come home, although I know that it won't be him, even though now that it is getting dark I cannot imagine who else it might be I look across at Naira who is staring out of the doorway into the gloom of the yard, and I see fear in her eyes. Her mouth hangs slightly open and she does not move. She looks so terrified I am afraid that she might drop the plates that she is holding, although that does not really seem important even while I am thinking it.

But these thoughts must have been over in a few seconds, because Maajid is instantly at the gate, and unbolting it and pulling it open. There is a man standing just outside, and although it is hard to make out anything in the gloom from where I am standing in the kitchen, I can make out the distinctive shape of the cap on his head and so I know that it must be a policeman.

For some reason, I don't expect to be able to hear what he is saying very clearly from where I am standing. Perhaps this is because it is dark outside, and because I am muddled and confused by everything that has happened, but he says 'You are Maajid Khan,' and I hear the words as loud as if they were being spoken in the room beside me. I hear also that it is not a question. And I can hear that there is something in the voice of this policeman, that tells me that he is angry at having to come here, and angry also that he has to speak to Maajid. He wants to get it over and done with, and does not care that Maajid and myself and Naira and anyone else who is around to hear, can tell that he resents having to speak to Maajid. And although he has not met Maajid before, already this policeman does not like him.

'I have come to tell you that your son is in the DRS hospital in Patna.' he continues, and when Maajid says quickly *what has happened to him?*' he ignores Maajid, and continues as though he does not hear him. 'He is still a prisoner, but if you wish to visit him it is permitted, and they will want money for his treatment.' And Maajid starts to ask him again what has happened but he has already turned away, and very quickly I hear the engine start up again, and the wheels spinning briefly on the road with a scraping, rushing sound, and then the sounds are disappearing into the night into the village into somewhere anywhere in infinite India and we are left standing in a huge and horrible silence that feels like a void.

'They have beaten him up and injured him and he is probably dying!' Naira suddenly wails, and I stand there wanting to contradict her because I am afraid that she will hurt herself again, but I know I also am thinking the same thoughts, that I have the same suspicions. Also some small detached part of me of which I am ashamed is thinking that if Naira claws her face now, Maajid will see her do it. And then he will understand that what had happened a few days ago was as I had said it was. I say nothing for a moment, but Naira puts down the plates that she is holding, and I am fascinated by the very careful way that she bends down and places them gently on the ground and straightens up again and steps away from them and then I look away from her again and see that Maajid is standing just outside the doorway now, watching her. Her face is expressionless and she appears calm but in the lamplight her eyes seem suddenly to glitter and widen as she steps deliberately towards the fire and I cannot move, my eyes are on her and I watch as she places both her arms into the flames and for a moment stands there without moving and without her face so much as twitching.

I am horrified and terrified and I cannot move and Maajid cannot move and then suddenly she throws her head back and shrieks with pain and at the same time Hana is rushing into the kitchen and screaming Mama, Mama, Mama, what is Naira doing? No, Naira, no! Stop it! And she bursts into tears and instantly it feels as though I have been released from an evil spell and I step quickly forward and grab Naira's arm to pull her from the flames and at the same moment Maajid is beside her and he grabs her other arm and drags her away out into the courtyard and says Oh merciful Allah! What have you done, woman?

I stand for a moment beside Hana who is still weeping, and I put my arm around her shoulders, and draw her to me. Her face is buried in my dress, but I can still hear her muffled sobs, and I am whispering to her and telling her that it is alright, that everything is alright, but it is not, and Hana knows that it is not, and oh, what are we to do?

Out in the courtyard, Naira is standing looking down at her arms, with a look of horror on her face. I cannot see what they are like from where I am standing, and I wonder confusedly where Maajid has gone. But then he is back, and he is leading Naira out into the street, and I hear the sound of the pump and Naira is gasping and sobbing, and I can hear the gushes of water and Maajid is speaking, although I cannot hear what he says.

And now Leila is also in the kitchen, and she sees Hana crying and she must have heard Naira scream and everything that had happened, and I wonder briefly why she had not come in before. But now when I look again at her, I see in her eyes a look that is a little like the look that I saw in Naira's eyes. I know that it is fear, but she is not weeping and she says nothing, and I go cold and shiver and want to burst into tears, and I think oh what is happening to us all? This is so terrible!

I do not know how long Naira and Maajid are outside, but it seems as though the three of us have not moved when they return. Naira is weeping quietly now, and Maajid comes up to me and says gently 'Siddiqa, where is that bottle of balm? You know what I mean, the soothing stuff.'

I think oh yes, of course, and say 'It is on that shelf up there. Why did I not think of that?'

But he takes it down without another word, and gives it to me and then he says 'You had better go and help her.'

I gently remove Hana's arms from around me, and take the bottle and go out to the courtyard. Naira is sitting on the edge of the veranda, in the light of the lamp where we should have been eating supper. She watches me approach, with dull eyes and a face that now has no expression, and I squat beside her and say 'Let me put some of this on your arms.'

Still she says nothing, but she holds her arms out towards me, and I gasp as I see that her wrists are raw and blistered, and there is a pale watery liquid seeping from them, and in some places this is mixed with blood. I am suddenly afraid of touching them, and Naira seems to understand this for she says 'Please put some on, if it will ease the pain.'

I do not like to do it, but I do as she asks and as gently as I can, I smooth the fresh-smelling balm over her wrists. She gasps at first, but then she sits silently and I think that must take an effort, because I am sure that just my touching her must be painful, but then I am finished, and she says 'Thank you,' and then drops her head.

For a while I still squat beside her, and I want to speak to her, but I know that there is nothing that I can say. I find that I am looking down at the hand that I have used to put on the balm, and I am staring at the blood that is smeared on my hand. It is a foolish thought, but it is a phrase that people use, that her blood is on my hands. I am thinking again of what has been happening over the last few days, and I am also thinking over and over again in the privacy of my thoughts, that her blood is on my hands. It seems to be a long time before I get to my feet and go to wash my hands.

We will go and see Tariq tomorrow, but Maajid says that it will be best if Naira does not come yet, since we do not know what condition he might be in. And it might not be good for her to see him if he really does have any bad injuries, although we might be able to take her once we know.

***

I am dreaming. I am dreaming that Naira is a big, fat spider who is sitting at a loom and weaving a web. She is working so quickly with all of her arms or legs or whatever they are, that the web is cascading down off of the loom. After a while I see that there are men trapped in her web; there is Tariq, and there is another who I somehow know is Tariq's friend, although as far as I know I have never seen him, and there is Maajid and the girls, and now I am tangled in the web too, and I am struggling, but I cannot free my arms or legs. Now the great spider which is Naira has stopped weaving and is moving towards me, and its awful eyes are staring at me, and it is going to eat me and I open my mouth to scream and then I wake up.

It is dark and still and I can hear no sound other than Maajid's breathing beside me, but I feel uneasy and I imagine threatening creatures hidden in the darkness of the room. But I know that this is just the residue of my dream, and as I lie there listening to Maajid breathing softly I gradually relax, and then I am drifting off to sleep again.

And now I am a young wife again in Maajid's parents' house, and my dream becomes a confusion of shouting and angry faces, and I feel helpless because everything that I do is wrong. At first I am cooking, but I know that I have put the wrong spices into the meat and instead of saying something, I think that I will keep quiet and hope that no one will notice, but my mother-in-law comes into the kitchen and walks across to where I am standing and stirring the food. She looks at me suspiciously and immediately bends down to smell the cooking, then straightens up quickly and says 'Those are not the right spices! You have ruined the meal!' and I step back, scared, but I am too slow for she slaps me hard across the face and I fall down onto the floor.

When I shake my head and look up again, she has a huge bundle of clothes in her arms and she throws them down at me and says 'These all need mending! You were meant to have done those yesterday, you lazy slut, all you do is sit around and stuff your face with food.' She reaches down and grabs my arm and pulls it hard so that I have to stand up, although it still hurts me tremendously and I cry out, but she just says 'Pick up those clothes!' so I bend down to do so, but as I do there is a sharp pain in my side and when I turn around I see that she is holding a long sharp needle, and she is sticking it into my side and I can see the glee in her eyes as she does so and it hurts me terribly.

I think that I have spent a long time mending the clothes, because they are all in a neat pile, now, and I stand up because I will have other things to do, but I do not know yet what they are, so I stand still looking around the room uncertainly, until my mother-in-law comes into the room again and she says 'Well, have you finished yet?' '*I don't know*', I reply uncertainly and she is furious and grabs my hair and yanks it hard and now I scream, but she says 'Shut up!' And Maajid is in the room and she says 'It is night time, now, take her to your room' and I know that it is going to hurt because it always hurts and I think that it is because I am too young but it is no good my complaining, because my husband will do what he wishes so I begin to cry and I wish that I was still at home with my parents and my brother, but this is my home now.

And I feel myself falling down and falling, falling and she is still hitting me although I am falling and I hear shouting and all the family are shouting at me and now my father-in-law has come into the kitchen where I am again and lying on the floor and he looks at me angrily and as I look up at him I think 'Oh, that is Maajid. I thought that it was his father,' but he is still angry and I think now that he looks older than he should and then Tariq comes in to shout at me too, and I think that is not right. He has not been born yet but as I look down I see that my wrists are all burned and my hands are blackened and withered and I realize that I am really Naira and my heart seems to leap inside my chest and I wake up again.

I lie still listening again to Maajid breathing beside me, but I am thinking of Naira, because I cannot make my dream go away. Because the images are so vivid, and because it is so dark that I cannot make out any shapes in the room around me, everything that I see in my head appears to be so real. And because I am still sleepy as well as because of these other things, I feel that I cannot be completely certain of whether I am Siddiqa or whether I might not even have become Naira, but then I am thinking of a woman from this village who I had forgotten about, and now I cannot even remember her name, but she went away to a village on the other side of Kannapur to be a wife, where her new family lived on a tiny patch of land where they grew a few vegetables for the market. She seemed pleased to go, but the following year we heard that she had died after accidentally drinking weed killer, and then soon everyone was saying that her family were cruel to her and beat her constantly, and that she could no longer stand it. Obviously we do not know the truth of the matter, but her life must have been truly terrible if she really did choose to kill herself in such a dreadful way. And perhaps it is only the darkness and my mood, but I am not sure why I have thought of her again.

TWELVE

It seems that there are many hospitals in Patna, and it takes us some while to find the DRS. We are directed backwards and forwards across Patna near to the river, and we eventually find the hospital over towards the airport in a rather crowded area. At one point we are going along a huge, long road that is like a bridge crossing high over many buildings and other roads, and when I look over the side it is terrifying and Maajid calls back over his shoulder that it is a flyover. I have seen these in films, of course, but I have never crossed over one, and I wish I was back in our peaceful village and that everything was alright once more.

Once we are at the hospital, Maajid parks the motor bike and we find the entrance and go in, and then he begins to ask people where we can find Tariq. All of the corridors are dark, and it is difficult to follow directions. Although some of the doorways are fitted with doors, many of them are simply covered in dirty hanging cloths, which add to the gloom. Other corridors branch off here and there, and there are no signs, and everything smells stale and unpleasant. After about a quarter of an hour we are directed towards some stairs, and told to go up to the next floor because that is where most new arrivals will go, and someone up there will be able to tell us where to find Tariq.

As we climb the stairs I am surprised to see that there is washing hanging on lines above our heads; there are a few bedsheets, but most of it appears to be everyday clothing and some of it cannot have been there long because although it is quite warm now, there are still quite a few puddles of water on the stairs and as we pass underneath a single drip falls upon my head. The walls around us are covered in grimy, grey and brown peeling paintwork that is flaking off of the crumbling plaster, while the windows are covered in filthy fly screens. I think that this is the first time that I have been inside a hospital, and I suppose that I had expected a new, clean building such as we see occasionally on television.

The second doorway that we look through opens into a small room with four beds in it, but only one of them is occupied. A man lies under a sheet, and his face is cut and bruised and partially covered in bandages, so that it is only when Maajid walks softly right up to the bedside that he realizes it is Tariq, and I see him stiffen and he beckons me over. When I reach the side of the bed, I am shocked at the sight of Tariq. He is awake and says 'Hello. It is good to see you. How did you know that I was here?'

They can't have thought that there was any danger of Tariq discharging himself from the hospital, for there was no sign of any police. I had expected to see a uniformed policeman sitting on a chair beside his bed, with one of those huge, heavy rifles on his lap, just like the guard that usually sits inside the entrance to the bank in Kannapur and, for all I know, every bank in India. The doors are usually half open, and held that way by a big chain. The guard is on his stool just behind one of the doors, so that you do not see him until you enter the building, but as you do, he sees you. The rifle…it always seems so much larger and heavier than I imagined it would be. When we were children, and played at soldiers or robbers or whatever my brother decided that he wanted to be at the time, he would pick up a long stick to serve as his rifle, and that seemed large enough to me. But the real thing, well, that seems almost unbelievably huge. I imagine it firing, and the sound that it would make is a massive, terrifying explosion. Just the sight of it is frightening.

'The police came and told us last night.' says Maajid. 'What happened to you? Are you hurt badly?'

'Not as badly as it looks, I think, although bad enough. I've been told that a couple of my ribs are cracked and my arm is broken, but, strangely, it doesn't feel too painful, although it hurts if I take a deep breath. Maybe it will later. I have got to have some more x-rays, but they won't do them until we pay for them, I'm afraid. I've no idea where my wallet is; they took everything off of us at the police station. Can you pay them?'

'Of course.'

'Thanks. As to what happened, I suppose I ought to tell you the whole story. It looks as though the police beat me up, but it wasn't that.'

'Then it can wait.' I say. 'I think you should rest.' But Tariq shakes his head and looks anxiously at me.

'No,' he says. 'I want to tell you. I need to tell you. It may help me to get everything clear in my own mind. I was stupid. I should never have gone out, but I was so angry that I didn't think.' He stops to catch his breath for a moment, and then carries on.

'I didn't want to believe Naira, and so I was going to speak to Satyak as my friend. I was certain that he would reassure me that nothing had happened, or that even if it had, that Naira had led him on. I wanted to believe that. But when I got there I found I was more suspicious of him than I had realized, and I also saw something in his eyes that made me think maybe Naira had been telling the truth. Then I thought to myself 'My friend has betrayed me!' and the next thing I knew I was shouting at him.' Again he stops, and he winces and closes his eyes for a moment.

'Can't this wait?' I ask, anxiously, but he opens his eyes again and looks at me.

'I must tell you,' he says, simply. 'Please let me continue. So...' he thinks for a moment 'I was telling Satyak that Naira had told me what he had done, and instead of denying it, he said 'what do you expect if your wife is out walking the streets in the dark? She must have no respect for her husband or his family. I shall not allow my wife to do that when I am married. A wife's place is indoors, in her husband's house.' And this made me feel most angry so that I did not care that his neighbours could hear us, or that his parents then came out from the house, and I said it was not yet dark and you can have no respect for me as your friend, if you would do a thing like that and he laughed and said 'oh, it was only Eve Teasing, what does it matter?'

'Well, that made me feel angrier still, and I went to hit him but he was expecting that and jumped back into the doorway, and his father told me to go home or he would send for the police, and I said something about Satyak being the one who would end up in a police cell and made a quick lunge for him and just managed to grab his shirt. Then we were fighting on the ground, and I know it was stupid, Father, but I had become really angry, and really wanted to hurt him, but it seems that someone must have already sent for the police, or perhaps they were just nearby anyway, for a jeep roared up out of the darkness and a couple of them jumped out and pulled us to our feet and bundled us into the back and drove off.' Again he has to pause to get his breath back, and this continues all the time he is talking, although I will not keep interrupting him to tell you this.

'At the police station they were quite rough with us, but when they found out what we were fighting about their moods suddenly changed. They seemed to find it all very funny and they gave Satyak a cigarette and I had to listen while they were saying things like 'was she any good, then?' and Satyak didn't seem to know what to make of this sudden change and he sat smoking the cigarette and looking down at his feet, and when he didn't seem to want to answer, they became cross with him and their moods changed again, and one of them slapped him across the face, knocking the cigarette out of his hand, and said 'you know that rape is a capital offence, don't you?' and he looked up quickly then, and I could see that he was suddenly afraid and he said 'I haven't raped anyone.' Then one said 'Oh, so she wanted you to do it, did she?' and so he said 'No, I didn't do it!' 'Oh so this man is lying, is he? Or did the woman lie?' and I wanted then to say that I wasn't accusing him of that, that Naira had told me that he had assaulted her, but that nothing else happened, although I suppose that if he hadn't been interrupted then it might have, but I was too afraid to speak.

'They took him out of the room, then, and turned their attention to me. 'Why was your wife out after dark?' they asked me. 'No decent woman would be out at that hour. Is she a whore?' And it went on and on, seemingly for hours. First they were telling me that Naira must have been asking for it, or that she went out deliberately looking for it, and then they changed their approach and accused me of lying, and then of taking a woman's word who was obviously lying, and then they said she must be a whore and that I was pimping her to my friends and I just seemed to be saying 'no' to everything that they said and then one of them said I must be a strange sort of man to get upset about a bit of innocent Eve-teasing and what sort of a friend was I anyway? And finally they locked me into a tiny cell and left me for the night.

'The next morning they must have been busy with something else because, apart from one of them bringing me something to eat, I was left on my own for most of the day. It was only sometime around the middle of the afternoon that one of them came to the cell door again, and said 'Your parents are making a nuisance of themselves here and we will take you to Patna and get you out of the way for a while, until we decide what to do with you both.' He went away again, and about half an hour later Satyak was brought, and my cell door unlocked, and I thought that they must be taking us then, but instead they pushed Satyak into my cell and locked the door again. One of the policemen then sat down on a stool beside the door with a grin on his face, and I suppose he was expecting us to start fighting or arguing again, but I thought it best to ignore Satyak, and he just sat down in the corner anyway, and avoided looking at me.

'Maybe they got bored with that, or perhaps they had another reason for putting us in together, but a while later they unlocked the door and took us outside and put us both in the back of the jeep, with a single policeman who sat all of the time with his rifle on his knee, staring out of the back. He didn't seem to want to look at us at all. I think the one who was passenger in the front had his pistol out, while the driver put his foot down and drove as if there were devils on our tail.' He paused. 'But the devils weren't behind us; they were up ahead, waiting for us.

'It was obvious they were all frightened, and I'm not surprised at that. I don't know why they decided to set off for Patna when it was already late afternoon. Everyone knows how dangerous it is. The roads were virtually empty long before we had even reached Jehanabad. I don't know whether Satyak was frightened of the bandits. Perhaps, like me, he was too busy worrying about what the police intended to do to us. I still didn't really know why they were taking us to Patna, anyway. But we joined the main road, went through Jehanabad, and after a while began to drive along the long, straight, stretch where the trees are right up to the edge of the road on both sides. It was much darker under the trees, and the driver had just put the lights on – I could see the glow of the rear lights where I was sitting – when boom! There was what seemed like an enormous explosion, and I was thrown violently sideways and everything went dark.

'I woke up with all sorts of pains in my body. My leg was twisted underneath me, which hurt like hell, and my head felt as though it had been kicked by a horse. But my wrists and arms were the worst; did I say they'd handcuffed our hands behind our backs? Well, that really hurt, now. The handcuffs were digging into my wrists and it felt as though they had cut me through to the bone. It wasn't completely dark, but I couldn't make out much. I think the bang on the head had affected my eyesight, anyway. But I was lying on the ground, and I couldn't work out where the jeep was. It seemed important to me at the time, but I could feel the ground underneath me and it felt empty all around – you know how you can feel if there's something near you even if you can't see it? Well, I couldn't, and couldn't make out what had happened to the jeep. But then there were voices, and suddenly what I assume was a gunshot that made me jump because it was so loud and terrifying – I thought that someone was shooting at me and I couldn't move. But nothing came my way for a while, and I heard the voices again; it seemed as though there were quite a lot of them, and I wondered if I should call for help.

'Next thing I knew, though, I was surrounded by men. They seemed to be talking to me, but I couldn't make out what was being said. I suppose I was concussed. But then a torch was shone on my face, and then it seemed to pass up and down my body, and what I suppose was a foot was suddenly pushed against my hip, and rolled me over so that I lay on my front, now, with my handcuffed hands behind me.

'When they saw that, it must have been obvious that I was a prisoner, and there was some more talking and I felt my head lifted gently and some water was poured in my mouth, which I drank greedily. I hadn't realized how thirsty I was! When they put my head down, it was resting on something soft, and then the torch was switched off and they just seemed to fade away into the darkness.

'I'm a bit confused as to what happened after that. I was unconscious some of the time, but at other times I was lying on the ground wide awake, very uncomfortable, in pain a lot, and very thirsty. I didn't know where I was for a while, or, at least, I had almost forgotten that we had been on the road, so I was surprised when I heard the sound of an engine approaching and a vehicle of some sort must have passed me about ten yards away. I saw a headlight as it approached, but once it had passed I couldn't move to watch it. I don't know whether the driver saw the wreck of the jeep, but he obviously wasn't going to stop. And who could blame him? It might have been a trap. I wouldn't have stopped if I had been him. But I didn't think like that at the time, and when he drove past without stopping I felt really angry, and I started swearing at him like an idiot. I was calling out all sorts of things, but then I seemed to just realize he had gone and I felt suddenly very tired.

'It became much colder. I've no idea how long I was lying there while the occasional vehicle went past, but then there was a very long time indeed when there seemed to be none. I kept hearing noises, though. Birds, some of them, and insects, and there must have been some other animals, although I never caught sight of them. I remember suddenly being very worried that a leopard might be attracted to the smell of my blood, and I couldn't think of anything else then for ages. Then I kept imagining that I heard voices, and I would strain my ears to listen but then when I did, it seemed that they had stopped again. Later on, the whispering started. I suppose I must have imagined it, but I began to hear whispers all around me. Maybe it was the night breeze, rustling the leaves, I don't know. I could never catch any words.

'And then it seemed that there were more birds singing; it definitely began to get louder. A few moments after I had noticed this, I could see that it must be dawn because although none of the light could reach me under the trees, I could now just make out where the road ran; I could see the space between the trees where I was lying and the ones on the other side of the road. I could also see the jeep, now, a dark shape not far from where I was lying. It was still quite a long while before the cars began to pass, though. An auto went past first, with one passenger, a big man in a peaked cap. Now that there was some light, it must have been obvious that the wrecked jeep was a police vehicle, and the driver slowed down and stopped and I could tell that they were staring at the wreckage. Neither got out, though, and I suppose that the big man, who was obviously a police officer, must have feared an ambush, and they turned around and sped off again, back the way they had come.

'After this, more vehicles began to go past. The first few drove past without slowing down, but then a motorcyclist came along. As he did so, he slowed down, went past, and then came to a stop some way up the road. I couldn't see him clearly from where I was lying, but after a moment he turned around and came back, and then stopped beside the jeep. I remember thinking that I had to call to him for help and I tried to lift myself up a bit to shout. I suppose that I must have exerted myself too much, because I must have become unconscious again, and I don't remember anything else until I felt myself being lifted and then I opened my eyes and I was being carried by a couple of men, very uncomfortably, towards the back of another jeep, one of a couple that were parked beside the wreckage of the one that we had been travelling in.

'I was thrown into the jeep, and the men who had been carrying me, who I now saw were police, climbed up in the back as well and then the engine started up and we set off. No one spoke to me, and although I was in quite a lot of pain I felt too frightened to speak to them. I wasn't offered anything to drink, and they did not try to take off the handcuffs. I suppose in their eyes I was still a prisoner. And, you may not believe it, but now it was the first time that I wondered what had happened to the others who had been with me in the jeep – Satyak and the police.

'I think that I had expected to go back to Kannapur, or, at least, I would have done if I was thinking straight at the time, but we went on to Patna. It was as if they were determined to take me there, no matter what happened. When we got there, and the ride there seemed to go on forever, although I suppose that was because I felt so bad, I was taken into a little room with one small, high window and sat in a chair and then they all left the room. I was only left alone for a few moments, though, because the door opened again and a sergeant came in accompanied by a man who turned out to be a doctor. He examined me carefully; prodding me and asking repeatedly which bits hurt, and put various plasters and bandages on me and then said that I would have to go to hospital. I don't think that the sergeant liked that at all, because he frowned and then glared at me and said to the doctor I think that we had better have a word outside and they left the room.

'They were away for some time and I suppose the doctor was having a hard time of convincing the sergeant, but eventually two policemen came in and said come with us, you are to go to the hospital, so I stood up and turned round and said can I have these off? and showed them the handcuffs. One of them laughed then, although he didn't look particularly amused, and just said maybe if we knew where the key was, and then they led me outside and into another jeep and brought me here. It was much later, after a doctor had seen me, that someone came in with a hacksaw and got the handcuffs off. That's where some of these cuts have come from; he wasn't particularly gentle, and I suppose that he'd never had to do it before, but at least they're off now. I asked the doctor whether he knew what had happened to the others, but he just said I don't know anything except that you were in an accident. How long will I be here? I then asked him and he said until you're well enough to go back to the police station and then I didn't really want to ask any more questions, but just before he went I said wait a minute, did they bring anyone else in here from the accident? And he said I think a police officer came in this morning, meaning yesterday morning now, of course, but I said no, it would have been someone else. His name is Satyak but the doctor said no, there is no one of that name here. Are you sure? No one else came in today he said.

'I haven't seen anybody since then, other than someone who brought around a basket of snacks. I had a few packets of this and that from him, and I need to pay him for them, too. But I'm not really hungry at the moment. Perhaps you could leave me some money, though. I think that I've been asleep a bit, so I suppose that the doctor might have been back, or somebody else come in, but I wouldn't have known.' He paused, and then said; 'I think that I need to say sorry to Naira.'

THIRTEEN

We find a doctor and Maajid pays him for the x-rays that Tariq will need, and for the treatment that he has already had. Then, once the doctor has assured us that he will not be discharged back to the police for several days, we return to Tariq to say our goodbyes and tell him that we will come back again in a day or two. As we ride back through Patna, Maajid buys a paper from a vendor at the side of the road, and then a few sweets from another who waits at some traffic lights. 'I am sure the girls would like these,' he says. It seems a long time after, but I expect it is only about half an hour later that we are finally leaving the city behind us, and beginning to see fields alongside the road.

As we are driving along the long, straight stretch that Tariq had described to us, we reach a spot where there is a large pothole in the road and, a few feet away under the trees, a jeep lying on its side. Maajid slows to a stop, and we both sit staring at the wreckage without speaking. We must have passed it on our way to Patna, but it is common to see wrecked vehicles here and there along the road and we obviously did not then realize its significance. From where I am, I can see the top and the front of the jeep, and I realize that it must have turned over at least once to have ended up in that position. The cover has disappeared, so I can see that both of the front seats have been destroyed, the bonnet is bent open, and both of the front wheels have been blown off.

I am shaking, now. I feel cold and I feel tears running down my cheeks. But, before I can say anything to Maajid, a policeman appears from amongst the trees. He frowns and waves at us to go away and so, with a quick look around, Maajid drives off.

We are home again about two hours later. When Naira opens the gate to let us in, I see both Hana and Leila beside her, and they come running over as Maajid parks the motorbike and we get off. 'Mama, Mama, how is Tariq?' and, 'Shall we tell them what has happened?' they shout.

'Wait,' says Naira, 'how is Tariq, first?'

'What has happened?' asks Maajid, immediately. Hana rushes over to the corner of the yard beside the kitchen and points to a large, heavy rock.

'This was thrown at the house, Baba,' she says.

'No one was hurt,' says Naira, quickly. 'It landed on the roof of the veranda just outside the kitchen, and made a loud bang, but didn't hit anyone.'

'Who threw it?' I ask.

'I don't know. I didn't want to go outside to look.'

'No, quite right,' says Maajid, calmly, although I can see that he is shocked. He bends down and picks up the rock, and then stands looking at it, and no one speaks for the moment. Then he looks up at the roof, thoughtfully hefting the rock up and down in his hand, as though he might be working out an enemy's strength. 'Tariq is being looked after in the hospital,' he says to Naira. 'We've left some money for his treatment.' He hesitates, and then continues. 'He was being taken to Patna when the police jeep crashed. He has a couple of fractures, but he is not in any danger.'

'What is a fracture?' asks Leila and Hana says it is another way of saying a broken bone. 'Oh,' says Leila and looks scared.

'He will be alright,' I say quickly to her.

'What is going to happen to him?' asks Naira.

'Do you mean when he is better? He is still in custody,' replies Maajid. 'I suppose they are still intending to ask him questions. I don't think they've charged him with anything, yet.'

'But they must have asked him lots of questions by now!' she exclaims. 'Did he tell you what had happened?'

'Only that they questioned both of them about the fight,' Maajid says carefully.

'Then why were they taking him to Patna?'

'I'm not really sure. Tariq says they were getting fed up with us going in and asking questions, but that doesn't really seem a good reason.' He shrugs. 'Who knows why the police do these things?'

'What about the other one?'

'The other one? You mean this Satyak? I don't know. Tariq says he hasn't seen him since the crash, and no one has told him anything.' He pauses. 'Either he is in a different part of the hospital, or perhaps in the cells at the police station. I don't know. But I am more concerned about Tariq,' he says, glancing at me. 'The doctor we spoke to says that they won't let the police take him away before he is better, but if the police took it into their heads to demand that he go with them, I don't suppose the doctor could stop them. We will go and see him again tomorrow or the next day.'

'I want to come next time,' she says immediately.

'No,' he replies, 'your place is here. Someone must be here in case we are delayed for any reason, anyway, otherwise the girls will not be able to get in from school.'

***

Maajid has no work again the next day, and as soon as the girls have gone off to school he gets up from his chair and says 'I think I need to go and stretch my legs,' and he opens the gate and goes out. I am left with Naira who is very quiet again this morning, and has not eaten any breakfast - although I don't suppose that she will waste away, I think to myself. It is unusual for her not to have made sure that she has had a good meal, though.

Naira is outside at the pump with the breakfast pans and dishes when Maajid returns. He comes up to me quietly and says 'There is something in the newspaper that I think you ought to see, but I'd rather Naira didn't know yet. Let's go to our room,' and he turns again and walks slowly across the yard towards our room, for all the world as though he were going to fetch his shoes or the bike keys. I stand still for a moment, conscious that Naira might see us through the gate from where she is working, trying to think of a reason why I might be going to our room but then I smile to myself and think there might be many reasons why I would be going to my room, now, and whatever it was I would not be needing to explain to Naira, so I follow him inside.

He is standing holding the newspaper which is opened at one of the inside pages and folded in half. 'Do you want me to read it?' he asks me, uncertainly, and at any other time I would be amused because he knows perfectly well that I can read, but there is still a part of him that assumes that no woman of my age in a village would be able to.

'No,' I say, 'just let me see. What do you want me to look at?'

'This bit,' he says, pointing at a couple of paragraphs at the side of the page. The headline says simply 'Bandits blow up police jeep murder police'. Then it goes on to say that a bomb was laid in the road to target the police and that a jeep on its way to Patna was blown up, and that the three police on board were killed. It says two of them were killed by the explosion, but the third one was shot at close range, and that the Naxalites are assumed to be responsible. There is no mention of anyone else being in the jeep.

'It does not mention Tariq or the other.' I say doubtfully.

Maajid shrugs and says 'It would be quite a coincidence if there had been two separate instances like that on Monday night. And Tariq told us that there was a gunshot, didn't he?'

'I don't remember; there was so much. But why doesn't it mention the two boys?'

'Maybe the newspaper people didn't think it important. Maybe the police didn't tell them. I don't know. But I do wonder where this other boy is. Perhaps the bandits have taken him; they do sometimes take people and ask for a ransom to return them.'

'But why just him? Why wouldn't they take Tariq, too?'

'I don't know,' he replies, and hesitates, but then continues.' Do you know what I think? I think this other boy is dead, too. That's why he isn't in the hospital. I think I ought to go and see his family to find out what they have heard.' I think of the rock that landed on the roof the previous afternoon while we were out.

'No!' I say, quickly, but he seems to realize what I am thinking.

'We don't know that was them,' he said sharply. 'I doubt they know anything about what's happened. I think if they'd had a visit from the police, we would have heard from them by now. I wonder whether we should have gone straight away and told them what Tariq told us. If they think that we are deliberately keeping information from them, it won't help things between us. I think I should go to see them now to share at least most of what we know and, if they still haven't been told anything officially about their son, I will offer to go to the police station with them again.'

I do not like this idea, but I suppose that he is right - and he has gone before I can think of anything that I might say to make him change his mind. But he is back again less than half an hour later, saying that Satyak's parents don't seem to be at home, and he was wary of asking their neighbours if they knew where they were, because he didn't want to draw too much attention to himself. Their neighbours are all Hindus, he continues, and there is tension in the air. He will go and try again later in the afternoon.

It is probably about an hour after we have finished our lunch, when suddenly there are gunshots and shouting in the distance. Naira drops the mugs that she is holding, and they clatter loudly on the ground and spew their dregs around by her feet. I can hear her gasp above those sounds; her hands are at her mouth and her eyes are wide open in fear. As I stare at her, I realize that my eyes, too, are wide like hers, and my mouth is hanging open. There is a sudden noise at the gate and now I, too, gasp and turn around to see Maajid pushing the bolts across to secure the gate. Then he turns towards us and says 'Quickly! Get indoors!' He ushers us up onto the veranda and then into our room, and we stand there looking at each other and not yet speaking. All I am thinking is that the girls will still be in school so they are safe, and whatever it is that is happening the girls are safe.

Outside, now, there is a silence that is almost more frightening than the gunshots and the shouting. For now there are no clues as to what might be happening, or whether it might be an incident that is now all over (although if it is, then whether it has ended in unspeakable tragedy, or whether all of the participants are safe, we do not know). But it might be just the beginning of something dreadful - maybe even now there are bandits stalking through the village looking for victims...even now they might be approaching our gate, and it would never keep out a determined intruder...and I want to scream now because I am certain that they are coming and I feel myself tensing and I know my nails are digging into the palms of my hands and I am going to scream I know that I am going to scream and then 'shush,' says Maajid softly, and he takes one of my hands and draws me gently to his side and I relax slightly, although I am still most fearful.

And still there is silence outside, but now I think that all of our neighbours must be hiding in fear like we are, and that is why I cannot hear anyone. But even as I think that, I hear a voice somewhere outside. And then another. And very soon it seems that everyone is speaking, and I think that I have never heard so much talking. We look at each other again and then without saying anything we all go to the gate. After a moment's hesitation, Maajid slowly unbolts it. We open it and peer out cautiously, and see little knots of people talking, so we go and join the small group nearest to us who are standing around the pump. One is saying 'No, I don't think so. It sounded more like it was very close by.'

'Gunshots always sound very loud,' says another, knowledgably, 'They might have been further away than you think.'

'Well what about the shouting? Did you hear what they were saying?'

'No.'

'They were threatening to kill everyone,' says another.

'Are you sure?'

'Yes, yes, I'm sure of it.'

'But who were they?'

'I don't know. Bandits, certainly.'

'Not the police?'

'Not the police.'

'Did you see anything?' There is another group of people coming along the street now.

'No,' they reply, 'but it sounded very close by.'

'Where?'

'Just back that way.'

'We ought to go and look.'

'They might be still there.'

'There haven't been any more gunshots. They must have gone.'

'Or they're all dead.'

'They might be. Someone ought to go.'

'Has anyone gone for the police?'

'I don't know.'

After a while, the men begin to move slowly back up the street and, after a quick glance at me, Maajid goes with them and Naira and I go back through the gate and I turn round to close it behind us. As I turn back again, I see her go into her room and drop the curtain down behind her. After standing in the middle of the yard for a moment, staring at the curtain, I go into the kitchen to boil some water.

Once the chai is made, I go to call Naira. There is no reply, though, and now I am standing on the veranda and wondering whether she has decided she doesn't want to speak to me, or whether perhaps she has just fallen asleep. I hesitantly call her again, a little louder this time, but again I hear no reply. I stand there a short while longer, and then begin to feel embarrassed by my indecision, as well as a little bit angry, which I don't really understand, so I put the mug down on the veranda beside the doorway, and go into our room to see what the time is, thinking that the girls will be due back soon. I also wonder how long it will be before Maajid returns.

I go back to Naira's doorway, and this time I call her more loudly. I hear some rustling noises, and after a moment or two she pulls aside the curtain and says 'Sorry, Amma, I was suddenly very tired.' I can see she has been crying and I wonder why I am finding it so difficult to feel sympathetic, so I just leave her with the chai and go across the yard into the kitchen without saying anything further.

I am looking through the jars and tins for the spices that we shall need for supper, when Naira comes in with the empty mug. She smiles slightly at me, and puts the mug down beside the fire. Then as she stands up and turns to go out again, I say 'Oh, Naira, since you're here, can you get the mustard seeds and the cardamoms down from the top shelf for me?' and I point at the jars at the end nearest to where she is standing.

'Of course,' she says, and reaches up to take them both down, but one of them seems to slip through her fingers and as she makes an unsuccessful grab at it, she drops the other one. They both land heavily on the ground and although the floor is only of beaten earth and dung, one of them smashes to pieces and mustard seeds and shards of glass fly across the room.

I have jumped backwards without thinking and only narrowly avoid falling over the sack of onions, but I stumble slightly anyway, and now I am furious and I scream at Naira that she cannot do anything right and as well as breaking the jar there are now mustard seeds all over the floor and there will be pieces of glass amongst them so that we cannot even collect them up again and use them, but they must all be thrown out. I take a deep breath and then say 'You can clear all of this up, Naira, and then go and get some more mustard seeds. We will need them for the supper.' And then I go out of the kitchen, across the yard and into our room where I throw myself down on my bedroll and lie there thinking no matter what she does or what happens to her she just seems to make me angry.

As I lie there I can hear through the doorway, even with the curtain across, the sounds of sweeping coming from the kitchen. After a while this ceases, and then after another few minutes I hear the gate opening and closing, and then it is quiet again. I wait a minute or so more then I get up, go to the doorway to push aside the curtain, and stand there looking out into the yard and at the gate. And now my mood seems to change again, and I realize that I am worrying about something, although I am not sure what it is. But, as Allah knows, we have plenty to worry about, I smile grimly.

It has become cloudy, and the sun has disappeared. The air has turned heavy and thick, and seems almost to taste bitter, and I think oh, that must be the reason for my mood. And as I think this, a sudden cold gust of wind makes me shiver, and stirs the dust in the yard, blowing it up in the air around me, so that I have to shut my eyes for a moment. When I open them again, I look up at the sky and this time I see that the clouds are moving quite quickly, and some of them are thick and deep and very dark. It looks like we might be about to get more rain, which doesn't happen very often here at this time of the year, but now it will be the second time in just a week. It will be most welcome if it comes, and I wonder that this thought doesn't make me feel happier than it does.

Now a few drops of rain do indeed begin to fall. At the moment they are not many, but they are big and heavy just like they were the other night. I stand in the middle of the yard, and I watch them splash on the ground; they are so big, that when they hit the ground, they burst into smaller, tiny, drops of water, and bounce back up into the air, mingled with little puffs of dust.

When they land again, they have become tiny blobs of mud and as more and more of them appear around my feet, they begin to join up together. I am beginning to get wet, but I am oddly fascinated by the lake of shallow mud forming around my feet, and cannot tear myself away. Perhaps we will have a thunderstorm again, and if we do I hope that Maajid will be back before it breaks and still I am getting wet, but then there comes the sound of Daanish's auto outside and I hurry to open the gate.

No sooner do I have the gate half open, than the girls rush in through the gap and onto the veranda and into their room. They have disappeared even before the sounds of their footsteps and the little chorus of 'Hello Mama' has faded away, and all I can hear after the auto has driven off is the rain beating down upon the roof. I am now getting very wet, and I shut the gate quickly and follow the girls into their room.

I am still there asking them about their day, and finding out whether they have homework to do, and the rain is still drumming down upon the roof, and splashing outside in the yard, when I catch a movement out of the corner of my eye. I glance up and, through the doorway, I see the gate open and Maajid comes in. He pushes the gate closed again, and stands still for a moment in the pouring rain looking around. Clearly, he is already soaked through and is making no attempt to hurry into shelter. I wave at him, but the sky is so dark and gloomy that there is little light in the room where I am standing, and he doesn't seem to see me. I call out, but again he doesn't hear me above the rain, and walks across to the kitchen. 'I'll be back shortly,' I say to the girls, 'You start your homework, and I'm sure that Baba will come and see you soon. He will want to change and get dry first, though.'

I run along the veranda and into the kitchen, to find Maajid standing beside the fire. He is already drinking a mug of chai. He looks at me as I enter, and I am relieved to see him smile faintly at me, but then I see that the smile does not touch his eyes.

'What has happened? Did you find out?'

He does not answer me at first, and then he says 'Yes, I found out.' Pause. 'We ended up at the place where Satyak's family live, and the police were there. There was a jeep parked further up the street from the house, and there were half a dozen policemen standing around talking to each other and to Satyak's father. There were other groups of people standing around too, but there was no sign of any violence. I think that I was expecting to see bodies on the ground, but everything seemed to be perfectly calm.

'But I thought I don't like this. Satyak's father's looked shocked, and as I looked at him he took a couple of steps backwards until he was leaning against the front wall of his house, and he was watching the police officer who was still standing in front of him. It looked as though he was watching his face closely, but although the police officer was speaking to him and pausing every now and again as if he was waiting for an answer, and then speaking again, Satyak's father was no longer speaking. He was only watching the policeman's face, and shaking his head from side to side as if trying to shake off something disagreeable. Then as I watched him, he turned suddenly and rushed through the doorway back into his house.

'Although the door was still open, the police didn't attempt to follow him. They continued to stand around and smoke and talk to each other, and with some of the onlookers, and I wanted to go and find out what had happened. I was afraid that I already knew, though, and I was afraid that if I was right, then there might be all sorts of repercussions. I decided to wait nearby, and try to find out once the police had gone. So I waited for a while, and it seemed that eventually the police just lost interest and got into the jeep and drove off. I went back to the house then, but I was unsure whether I ought to go in. Just then Satyak's father came out again, with one of his neighbours, and he came over and told me what had happened.' Maajid pauses again, taking a gulp of his chai. 'It wasn't as bad as I had thought, but still quite bad. The police hadn't come to tell him that his son was dead, but had said he was in the hospital in Jehanabad. They also told him that Satyak had been taken there by the bandits that had blown up the jeep, and because of that they think that he might be involved with those fellows. It seems the bandits also left money with the hospital for his treatment; quite a lot of money. He is badly hurt, although I don't know how badly.'

'But,' I say, 'why did they only take him to the hospital and not Tariq?' Maajid shrugs.

'I've no idea. Perhaps because Tariq is a Moslem and this other boy is a Hindu. I don't know. The police have said that they are going to arrest Satyak as soon as he is able to leave hospital, and they seemed to make it clear that they suspect him of being one of the bandits and that the jeep was blown up just to rescue him. Which is ridiculous, of course, because the bandits couldn't have known that he was in the jeep – unless the police think that one of their officers is an informer, of course.'

'What about his father?' I ask.

'Well, he is upset and angry and weeping as you would expect, of course. He was not at all happy to see me and was shouting that all of this was our fault, the reason that his son was injured and would probably die, and now they were going to arrest him again. He said that if Naira had not accused Satyak then none of this would have happened. I thought there was going to be trouble, but he began weeping again, and his neighbour then pushed him back inside the house. I thought that I'd better leave, then, because some of his other neighbours were beginning to mutter about us, and they were not looking very friendly.' He sighs. 'I wanted to say how sorry I was about his son, but he would not listen and he would only think that I was admitting that it was our family's fault, anyway.

'And now I am wondering whether we might not be wise to go and stay with my brother for a while after all. I do not need to remind you of what can happen when Hindu and Moslem begin to accuse each other of bad things.'

And indeed I go cold when he says this, knowing that the rock thrown at the house while we were out earlier could simply be the start of the trouble. There could be more to come; I know in my heart that there *will* be more trouble, and I know that Maajid knows it, too. Oh, why did we choose this woman for Tariq? I think to myself, but I do not say it out loud.

'What was the shooting about?' I suddenly remember that was how this all started this afternoon. Maajid smiles grimly.

'That really *was* the bandits! They arrived at the house before the police did, to tell the family about the boy. I don't know whether the police knew that, although I'm sure somebody has told them about it by now. If the police had turned up a few minutes earlier they would have run into them, and then there would have been real trouble. I don't know why they had to do all the shooting; I suppose it was to impress people.' He sighs. 'It seems rather stupid to me.' We look at each other without speaking for a few moments.

I will go and change,' he says then and goes out, leaving me staring after him. Eventually I follow him outside, intending to go to see how the girls are, to see whether they have started their homework. As I walk along the veranda, I remember that I have sent Naira out, and she will have probably been caught in the rain, but I shrug and say to myself I didn't know it would rain. She has probably managed to take shelter somewhere.

Hana is working on her maths homework, and I am watching her, and Leila is lying on her back reading a book that she is holding up in front of her face, when Maajid comes in through the doorway. With cries of 'Baba, Baba!' the homework gets pushed aside, and the book thrown down, and the girls are hugging their father, and I am smiling again, and the rain sounds as though it is stopping. Suddenly, everything seems to be normal again, and Maajid is asking Hana about her homework. She is explaining about the sums that she is doing, and Maajid looks at her in mock horror and says 'Oh, you are so much cleverer than your poor father. I do not understand anything of what you are doing. Does your mother understand it?'

'Yes!' she squeals, delightedly. 'Mama understands.'

'Oh,' he says, again. 'Then she must be cleverer than me, too.'

'I am glad that you realize it, at last.' I laugh.

'Are you really cleverer than Baba?' asks Leila, her eyes wide.

'Of course,' I reply, smiling at Maajid.

'We'll discuss that another time,' he replies, pretending to be hurt.

'Where is Naira?' asks Hana, then.

'Oh, she has gone out to the market.'

'In the rain, Mama?'

'It wasn't raining when she left.' I reply.

'When she gets back, you can tell her that we'll take her to see Tariq, tomorrow,' says Maajid.

'How will we do that?'

'We'll do what Tariq's boss does, and take an auto.'

'That's an awfully long journey,' I say, doubtfully.

'Oh, it's not that bad. We can go as soon as the girls have left, and we'll be back before they get home.'

'We will be alright,' says Hana.

'Oh, no,' I reply. 'You are too young to be at home on your own. We will have to lock the gates, anyway.'

'Oh.' She looks disappointed.

'I wasn't going to tell you,' says Maajid, 'but on my way back a couple of men spat at me in the street.'

'Who were they?'

'I'm not certain; neighbours or friends of that family, I suppose. I think…' he scratches his chin and stares across the yard '…I think that we must forbid Naira to go out on her own, for a while.'

'She is out now.' I remind him.

'Yes…' he continues to stare towards the closed gate '…when did she go out?'

'When? Oh, I don't know…half an hour ago? An hour?' He says nothing. 'It began to rain hard, remember.' I say, quickly. 'She probably took shelter for a while. She won't be long, I'm sure.'

'What had she gone out to buy?'

'Only some mustard seeds.'

'Well, that shouldn't take long.'

'No. It shouldn't.' Silence.

'The rain has stopped now,' he says eventually.

'Yes.' But even as we speak, I am aware that the skies have darkened again, and it looks as though we are going to get some more rain. Naira will surely hurry back, now, so as not to get caught in another shower.

But although we stand on the veranda in silence for another ten minutes or so, she does not return, and then the rain begins again.

'Come on,' says Maajid, at last, 'we must go out and look for her. I *am* worried, now. Bolt the gate behind us, Hana, and don't open it to anyone else until we come back. '

'Okay, Baba.'

'Where do we start?' asks Maajid, once we are outside and we have heard the bolt slide across behind us. 'Do you think she might have gone to her parents again?'

'She might,' I say. 'She might be anywhere. Let's go past the stalls just to make sure she isn't there.'

'Which way would she go to her parents?' asks Maajid.

'She would usually go along the lane where Satyak's family lives. But I don't suppose she'd go that way at the moment.'

'Let's go to the stalls, then, and then we can go the back way to her parents.'

It doesn't take us long to see that Naira is not at the stalls, but we stop anyway to ask whether she has been there to buy spices. We are told by one of the stallholders that Naira had been there about half an hour ago, but all she had bought was a length of cord. *Nothing else? No mustard seeds?* No, just the cord. *Which way did she go?* I didn't see.

And now we hurry on, going through a narrow alley between some of the poorer houses of the village, most of them little more than plastic sheeting and palm fronds over wooden frames. There seems to be no one around, and I think that most of the people here will be inside these poor shelters. I do catch a glimpse of a child crawling across the muddy ground inside one, through a gap where the plastic sheeting does not meet. And then we step past the last dwellings, and we are on the waste ground at the edge of the village, where on sunny days the children swing on the piece of rope that hangs from a branch of an old mango tree, and dig holes in the dirt, and play cricket. We will need to cross this and skirt around behind some more small houses to get to the area where Naira's parents live.

Despite the rain, there is an old man sitting with his back to one of the huts. He looks at us and his eyes narrow irritably, and then he waves at us to go away. It is the same gesture that the policeman used beside the wreckage of the jeep on the road from Patna. Go away. There is nothing for you to see here. I look at him, uncertainly, but Maajid suddenly runs forward with a cry and I look at him and then I see what he has seen and I stand there stupidly and watch him run over to the mango tree at the far side of the wasteland and I stare stupidly as he tries to lift the dead weight hanging from the branch and I stand stupidly as he looks desperately at me and shouts for me to help him but there is no point in my going to help him, I can see that from where I stand, although I take a couple of steps towards him before I halt. Apparently satisfied, the old man gets to his feet and wanders off into the rain.

GLOSSARY

Amma – Mother

ash – traditionally used to clean dishes after use. Mixed with a little water, they have a gentle scouring effect.

auto – autotaxi; the three wheeled taxi, common all over India

Baba – familiar name for father, the equivalent of 'Papa'

beedi – cheap cigarette made from tobacco and tendu leaf, tied with string at one end.

chai – spiced tea

chapatti – flat-bread made from flour and water

charpoy – cheap string cot

chips – potato chips, or crisps as they are known in the UK.

dal – lentil curry

dhobi wallah – one who washes clothes

Eve-teasing – euphemism for sexual harassment, the implication being that it is not serious.

Halal – Arabic word meaning lawful. When referring to meat, it means that the animal has been killed in a particular way.

lakh - unit of measure, equivalent to 100,000.

lungi – wrap around garment worn by men on the lower half of the body

masala – spices or spicy.

Naxalites – Maoist insurgency group. Known for carrying out armed attacks, mainly in rural areas, especially against the police.

paratha – fried flat-bread

puja – a religious ritual

wallah – one who performs a specific task (defined by caste)

ABOUT THE AUTHOR

Mick Canning was born in London, England, and lives in Kent, although he takes every opportunity to travel, especially to the Indian Subcontinent. 'Making Friends with the Crocodile' is his first published novel.

38286967R00090

Printed in Poland
by Amazon Fulfillment
Poland Sp. z o.o., Wrocław